EMPTY CITIES

MINUS AMERICA BOOK 2

E.E. ISHERWOOD

CONNECT WITH E.E. ISHERWOOD

Website & Newsletter:
www.eeisherwood.com

Cover Illustration by 'Covers by Christian'

Editing services provided by Mia at LKJ Books

ONE

Near Dulles International Airport, VA

Ted and Emily wasted no time in the residential home where they'd spent the night. They woke up with first light, picked out some food from the kitchen, gathered what little they had, and borrowed the family sedan to leave the neighborhood.

"Where should we go?" Emily asked once they were on the road.

Ted rubbed his throbbing temple; the crash yesterday only inflicted a few scratches, but he did have a nasty headache. "Eventually, toward help. We must report to any authority left and warn them Jeffries and his pals have the nuclear briefcase, possibly the codes. Right now, I have to make a stop. You'll see."

They were still close to Dulles airport, which he wanted to avoid, but he'd spent a lot of time thinking about this question last night.

Emily sat for a few seconds like she'd misunderstood him, then seemed to have enough of it. "Officer MacInnis, I'm the Vice President of the United States, I order you to tell me where we're going."

"President, actually," he said calmly.

She did a double take, then caught on. "Oh, you're being funny."

He snickered. "You said you liked to joke around. I'm playing the part of funny sidekick today."

She melted into her seat, as if glad she didn't really need to boss him. "I shouldn't have said that, actually. I do need to act more serious now. The nation is in crisis. Preventing more war is obviously urgent. Once I get in touch with someone in the military chain of command, I can let them know what's happened to the president and they can confirm my new rank. Hopefully, we can get some proper protection."

"What? Old Bessie and I aren't enough for you?" He patted his hip, where he kept one of the two pistols he'd taken from the White House. She still had the Sig Sauer P229 that John Jeffries had tried to kill her with.

When he'd touched the gun, he thought of his phone, so he pulled it out as he listened to her.

"I want an entire division of US Marines on the White House lawn pronto," she said while staring at the wooded country of northeastern Virginia. "That's when I'll feel safe."

He snuck a look at his phone.

To his surprise, Emily whipped her head around and caught him. "Hey! You're not supposed to text and drive. That's dangerous when you have a VIP on board."

He glanced at her to see if she was serious. She was.

Ted handed over his phone. "Will you tap voicemail? It says I have some messages. Might be Lieutenant Colonel Maxxon asking why I didn't bring his plane back to Andrews. Put it on speaker, so I can hear, okay?"

"I know how phones work, Ted. I just..." She held the device for ten or fifteen seconds, then leaned over to him and spoke with great reluctance in her voice. "Which button?"

Far from making him upset, he found joy in her lack of technical skills. She was supposed to be one of the premiere politicians in America— a woman he normally wouldn't chat up in a bar given her political bent. However, she'd turned out to be far different than her image, and her flaws made him like her even more.

"This one," he said with a grin.

She held it in between them so he could listen.

'Hello, and good day. This is Constitution One Banking. Your minimum payment is overdue. You will—'

"We'll get these calls until the power stops, I'm sure. Skip," he said while tapping the appropriate button.

"I'll do that," Emily complained. "You drive."

There were no other moving cars on the road, though there were lots of wrecks, and a few still smoldered from fires. When the people were sucked out of them yesterday, the cars themselves often drove for short distances. Most of them went into the nearby trees and yards of the suburban houses along the roadway, though a few came to rest in the middle of the lane. One or two crashed head-on with those coming from the opposite side.

His biggest fear at the moment was running into those convoys he'd seen the day before. While they both wanted to find friendly troops, nothing about the units on the road immediately after the attack had conveyed "friendly" to him. They seemed to operate with impunity even with the robot cat-things prowling the city.

The next message played.

'Ted. It's me. I'm safe here in Fairford. I heard...the plane you were in went down. I don't... I hope you're okay." The call ended.

"Who was that?" Emily asked with concern.

"My ex-wife," he said with mixed emotions. He'd not heard from her in years, but news traveled fast in the service. She was Air Force, too.

"Are you two..." she pressed.

"What?" He turned up his nose. "Hell, no. We split five years ago. Different career choices. That sort of thing. She's serving over the pond." He didn't want to talk about it.

"I'm sorry."

"It's fine. It tells us something important that we already suspected. England wasn't hit by whatever weapon wiped us out. That means we still have an ally out there."

The next message began, cutting off his train of thought.

"Hi, Uncle Ted. It's Kyla. Your niece—"

"Holy shit! She's actually alive!" He swerved the car in his excitement, then slammed on the brakes. He'd gotten about halfway onto the shoulder, but it was close enough. Belatedly, he realized he'd yelled over a good bit of the message.

"Play it again. Hit rewind. Please!"

Emily fidgeted with the controls but soon figured it out.

"Hi, Uncle Ted. It's Kyla. Your niece." She laughed nervously. "I guess you figured that out. I'm sleeping on board the ship tonight. I'm safe for now. I don't know why our phones aren't reliably connecting. The tech person here thinks a foreign power has hacked into some of the cell towers."

Ted used his knuckle to wipe away a tear filled with joy. He went a full day hoping she survived on the ship, though he'd pretty much accepted she was gone, like her mother. Now...

The message went quiet, and he thought it was over, but she continued in a lower volume. "I'm scared. A rumor has gone around that people on the outside have been killed, like they were here on the ship. Is that true? Is Mom okay, do you think? I haven't been able to reach her. Can you let her know I'm all right? I'll try to call you both again in the morning."

The line went dead. It was the last message.

Emily put the phone on the center console, but before she could do anything else, Ted threw his arms around her, disregarding all rank and decorum.

"She's alive!"

Poor Sisters Convent, Oakville, MO

Tabby stood at the back window, looking outside. She was struck by the beauty of the sunshine as it beamed through the trees and lit up the well-manicured landscaping of the convent and vineyard. A doe chewed at some leaves at the edge of the forest toward the back of the property, reminding her she needed to eat.

The delightful scene also confirmed what she'd hoped to be true last night: they weren't overcome with poison gas.

"Good-bye, little doe," she whispered before turning around.

The common room was well-lit this morning. Sun burst in from large windows all across the back wall. Sister Rose said the convent would provide a peaceful resting place for her and the kids. For the kids, that was true.

Peter and Audrey were still asleep on the same sofa. She thought it was cute how he held his new girlfriend—like he was still protecting her from anything bad. Tabby was less certain if their parents would approve of them sleeping in the same spot, but her job was tour leader, not parent, for the teens.

By contrast, she'd hardly slept. The youngsters were her responsibility, whether she liked it or not. That burden refused to let her sleep soundly like the others. Her goal had been to return them to their parents, but now that was impossible. Her mind struggled with the logic of it for most of the night.

"How can you sleep so well, knowing your parents are dead?" she thought.

Her parents had been evacuated during the disaster. She was sure of that. All she had to do was find the police cordon set up to protect the citizens of eastern Missouri; her parents would be waiting for her there.

Mom and Dad weren't like the other kids' parents. They wouldn't have been caught flatfooted and helpless. Dad was ex-military and a businessman who took pride in being prepared for any emergency that could befall the mine. It was those preps that had saved her. When disaster struck on the surface, no one would be more prepared to get to safety than him.

"Good morning," the kindly Sister Rose said in a soft voice.

"Hello, Sister." She took the offered coffee cup. "Thank you."

"You're welcome, child. I'm happy to be of service."

"We didn't get a chance to talk last night. I don't see any clothes dropped around here. Were you the only one living in this place?"

A cloud passed over the nun's otherwise cheery face. "I was not alone when God passed through this home. There were ten other sisters, but they were all taken. You do not see their clothing because I moved their belongings into their bedrooms."

"I'm so sorry," Tabby replied.

"You have seen many losses on the outside?" Sister Rose asked. "Like the cars crashed out front?"

Tabby gulped, not sure she liked where the conversation was going. "There are lost clothes all over Bonne Terre, where we're from. I've seen empty cars on the highways. We've also seen the...clothing of the children's parents."

Rose's eyes were hopeful for a moment, until Tabby failed to add to the story. "So, the children lost their loved ones..."

Tabby nodded grimly. "It makes no sense. What did we do different that kept us safe?"

The nun held a necklace of beads. "I've been praying for guidance every waking moment. The ladies were chatting in here, like always, when Abbess Mary Francis asked me to get some seeds from downstairs. I did as she requested, but when I returned, she was gone."

Tabby didn't know how that helped her. "Can I see what's downstairs? Maybe there's something down there which protected you?"

Sister Rose set her coffee down, inviting her to do the same. The pair quietly walked across the carpeted great room to the doorway for the stairs. It was already partway opened.

"I never closed it when I came up."

11

They made their way down a long stairwell reinforced on the sides with slats of wood. It reminded her of going into a bunker. Or a mine.

"What do you call this space? It's huge." The stairwell revealed a big chamber below as they neared the bottom.

"The order bought this property from a winemaker who went out of business. He had this cellar constructed as a place to store casks of wine, but as the story was told to me, he couldn't afford to build the dumbwaiter lift to get the wine down here and back up."

"And you were all the way down here?" The narrow stairwell was so tall she imagined they'd gone at least two stories underground.

"Yes. I was in the back, with the seedlings."

When they reached the bottom, Sister Rose pulled a string for a single bulb. It did little to illuminate the dank space.

"The kids and I were down in the Bonne Terre mine, as I told you last night. We were a lot farther under the surface than you, but there has to be a connection. If you were down here, and your sisters died up top, and I was down there..."

She purposefully skipped what that meant for the fellow students of Peter, Audrey, and Donovan. They'd just taken the elevator to the top. The kids still had hope their peers would be found.

"No, child, I'm afraid it's worse than that. God died for our sins once. Now he came back and took only the good souls he wanted. No amount of rock or soil could prevent him from taking us if that was his will."

Tabby looked at her sideways. "My dad says it wasn't a big deal for God to die for our sins. He said he would die for me without blinking an eye." She shuddered at the notion of laying down her life for the kids, but she'd do it. She was pretty sure.

Sister Rose seemed to get defensive. "I'm sorry you don't understand."

"You're saying we're the bad souls left by God?"

The nun bowed her head. "I don't want it to be true, but we are sinners, yes. It's the only explanation that makes sense. God died for humanity once, but he finally ran out of patience."

Tabby looked once more around the musty storage area, then glanced up the stairwell to the small door at the top. Rays of sunshine penetrated the first few feet of the tunnel, but nothing more.

"We've got to get going, Sister. Thank you so much for your hospitality. We've got to find my parents. They're with the evacuees, you see, and I have to find them."

She didn't want to stick around the nun, as nice as she was, because she clearly held onto a lie, and Tabby wanted no part of it.

"Where will you go?" Rose asked.

"North," she said aloud. *To my parents*, she added to herself.

TWO

On board the *USS John F. Kennedy*

"Just line up the front and rear sights so they're level, exhale a little to steady yourself, then pull the trigger, not the weapon."

Meechum handed the pistol to Kyla. Last night she'd also given her one of her Marine blouses, stripped of all the rank. As one of the only civilians left on board, the warrior woman said she needed to dress tougher, so she couldn't be mistaken for a civvy anymore. Having a gun helped dispel that non-military feeling, too.

"Sounds easy enough." She'd fired the same pistol in the hallway yesterday. Kyla still wasn't sure she'd hit anything, but she wanted to make sure the next time would be different. It was the pistol she'd used to shoot Ben as he tried to get away, but she was convinced that was luck.

Meechum had set up a firing range on the flight deck of the aircraft carrier. There were no flights going in or out, because most, if not all, the pilots had been killed yesterday. The wide-open space was now a gigantic, empty parking lot.

They were out of port and away from shore, but a thin, hazy line of land hugged the horizon to the west.

"Where do you think we are?" she asked.

The Marine frowned. "Don't worry about that. Worry about your M9." She gestured to the pistol.

Kyla took a moment to feel the weight and appreciate what it was, then she did as instructed. She positioned herself in front of the box-like target, lined up the front and rear sights, exhaled, then squeezed the trigger.

Her ear protection blocked out most of the pistol's report, but it was still loud.

"Nice!" Meechum yelled. "You almost killed a bad guy."

Kyla stood about twenty feet from the target. A black hole had appeared on the rectangular piece of paper, about six inches above the head of the man's outline.

"Again!" the Marine shouted.

Kyla repeated her routine, doing her best to squeeze the trigger without moving the gun off target.

"Yes! You hit the guy!"

Meechum slapped her on the shoulder. "Now empty the mag. Fire at will."

She brought the pistol back up. Kyla held it steady with both hands, then pulled the trigger a couple of times. Once she had the hang of it, she fired off however many bullets were in the ammo box. The magazine, as Meechum called it.

Finally, the pistol wouldn't fire.

"Great job, dudette! You hit the man one more time, right in the center of his chest."

She pulled back her headphones. "I missed the rest? How do you hit anything with this gun?"

The blonde-haired woman flashed a knowing grin. "Weapon. We always call these weapons, not guns. I had you fire them all to show you how each shot takes you a little further off target. You have to continually adjust every couple, or you might as well be firing at the sky. You'll see less of that when we train you up on the M27 rifle, later."

They both looked up into the hazy morning air. The white smudge of a contrail caught her attention. "Are planes still up there?"

Meechum looked at the same place. "You're asking the wrong girl. I don't know jack about what's going on outside this ship, but by the looks of it, there is something flying."

While they were looking up, the sound of a propeller caught her attention.

"What the hell is that?" she asked. Meechum heard it, too.

A warning claxon activated a second later, suggesting the arrival wasn't friendly.

They both watched as a car-sized airplane came up over the front of the carrier's deck. It was light gray, with long, thin wings. Its cockpit was an oval-shaped bulb, but there were no windows. A propeller drove it from the rear.

"Get down!" the Marine ordered.

She fell to the deck but craned her neck to keep watch.

It flew slow, like it wasn't afraid to be seen. It came across the number 79 painted at the front, then it soared about thirty feet off the deck and toward the back. As it went over the two of them, Kyla noted the plane was shaped a lot like a plus sign, with a thin fuselage to go along with the narrow wings. A black ball hung out the bottom, right in the center of the plus.

It banked to the left once it motored by.

"Run," Meechum insisted. "Over there!" She motioned for Kyla to head for the carrier's island. A hatch waited for her on the other side of the arrestor cables. The Marine got to her feet, and Kyla scrambled to catch her.

While they sprinted to safety, Kyla observed the drone still making a wide left turn, as if intending to swoop in for a second pass from the front.

Before they reached the hatch, another Marine came out with his rifle at the ready. "Get in there. Stay!" Meechum ordered her.

Carthager emerged a short time later and seemed to instantly absorb the situation. "The Marine who shoots it down gets double pay this month!"

Kyla stayed inside the door as more Marines came to the deck, apparently excited at the prospect of using their rifles. She leaned outside to see the plane begin its second pass, but she flinched when the rifles started cracking.

The drone made it about halfway down the deck before it veered to its right. The Marines continued firing until the little aircraft went off the far side of the deck, and closer to the water, as if deftly avoiding the bullets.

"Go! Go!" Carthager yelled.

The Marines took off for the other side of the deck. Kyla didn't know why, so she followed at a safe distance. The drone appeared in the distance, not far above the water. It was making an escape attempt.

Once they had it in their sights, the Marines fell to the deck or took knees to steady their aim and line up shots. For several seconds, the air was filled with thunderclaps of gunfire. Someone must have hit it, because the drone seemed to dip a wing for a few seconds. It didn't go into the water, however.

Kyla watched it head for shore, her ears buzzing.

She'd forgotten to put on her ear protection; the headphones hung around her neck.

"I've got to get better at this war stuff," she told herself.

Carthager gave her a disapproving scowl as he ran by.

"We've got to talk to the captain," the Marine leader yelled. "That should not have made it within a hundred miles of this boat."

Fairfax, Virginia

"This is where you live?" Emily asked as soon as she got inside his apartment.

"I didn't expect the VP of the United States would be dropping by today." Ted kept his apartment clean because he was a freak for organization, so her complaint couldn't have anything to do with his cleanliness. Before he took the flight to Europe, he'd made sure everything was buttoned up and prepped for his return.

"It's so small!" she gasped.

"Ah, every man's nightmare."

She looked shocked. "No, of course I didn't mean it as an insult. Your office is the sky. I had it in my head you lived in an airy apartment with lots of windows."

"Maybe if you ordered the president to pay me more money?" He laughed because that would never happen. Ted wasn't in it only for the money; the office in the sky part was what kept him going.

"I might be able to change that," she said, playing off the legitimate chance she might already be President Williams.

He'd brought her to his apartment so he could get some of his supplies. On the way, it occurred to him that every store in the city was open for the taking, but he wanted to avoid looting unless he had no other choice. Plus, it would take more time to find the stores he needed than to go to the one place where he already had everything organized and ready.

"Maybe you can reimburse me for these, too." He flipped a hidden lever on the underside of his wooden coffee table, which released the lid. His tools of the trade were inside.

"You keep guns in your living room?" Emily said as if he'd lit his hair on fire.

He laughed heartily. "I think what you mean, ma'am, is you keep guns in your living room, *thank God*."

"I didn't expect it, is all. I'm glad you have weapons we can use. I'll feel better knowing you've got my back." He'd been watching over her since the assassination attempt.

"Like before, you've got your own back." He handed her a tricked-out AR-15 with all the fancy furniture. "And you'll keep on doing it with one of these bad boys." It had a synthetic collapsible buttstock, honeycomb aluminum hand guard, lightweight pistol grip, and a long, black scope.

She held it with awe, then glanced down into the hiding place. "How many of these do you have?"

"Ma'am, I'm afraid you're going to need a warrant to ask that question."

They laughed together, but she stopped on a dime. "Must you keep calling me ma'am? I get enough of that from the generals and political types."

He stiffened. "It's an old habit from years in the Air Force. I'll try to ease up on it, but I can't guarantee anything."

"Do your best," she smiled. "Call me Emily. Now, are you going to tell me how many of these things you've got?" Emily pointed at his stash.

"I can't tell you," he deadpanned. "Seriously. I've lost count. I keep the rest of them in a storage locker in town. These four are my babies, though. These will be fine for us."

She playfully scowled at him for a moment, then gingerly set the rifle on the sofa cushions.

He went on. "I also have food, water, a bugout bag, radios, and a pallet of ammo. We'll grab what we can and get the hell out of here."

Emily sat next to her gun. "Where should we go? Washington's empty. I wonder if anyone made it to the new Government Relocation Facility."

"The what?" he asked as he pulled another rifle out of the case.

"It's top secret, but I'm bumping you up as of right now." She chuckled, but only barely. "The government put a nuclear bunker below a Best Buy up in Leesburg. The idea was the entire US government, Congress and Justices included, would retreat there when the threat of nuclear war was imminent."

"The president didn't make it there."

"No," she replied. "He didn't even make it down to the shelter below the White House, if we believe your man Ramirez."

"You think Tanager could still be alive? Ramirez would have no reason to lie about that, would he?"

"No, I don't think he's alive. I only wish he was."

They sat there in silence for a short time, but Ted didn't want to risk them getting into a funk. "I've been thinking on where we should go ..."

"Where's that?" she asked.

He thought of her teasing yesterday after the crash. "Help me stack these guns by the door and I'll tell you."

San Francisco, CA

Dwight Inverness woke up in the dark. He opened his eyes and saw almost nothing, save a lone EXIT sign several stories above him. It cast a lonely light through the metal staircase, down to his carboard bed.

He breathed in the fumes of life: his rotgut vodka, cat urine from all the strays nearby, and a little bit of vomit, courtesy of another good night of panhandling.

From outside, he barely heard his bird talking away.

"Are you there, Poppy?"

It didn't reply, but she was probably missing him, so he thought it was time to get up and get the evening shift started.

It took Dwight at least ten minutes to pull himself to a sitting position, get on his feet, then walk up the stairs. As a professional homeless man, he'd found this refuge after months of living in less favorable places in downtown San Francisco. One day, while looking through trash in the alley, he noticed the security door of the skyscraper was propped open, so he went inside.

For shelter, it was perfect. He could hide downstairs in the mechanical room and never be bothered again. For weeks, he went in and out with no issues at all. He'd brought in his bed and stash of personal effects. He had even scored a small solar-powered flashlight, which often gave him enough light to help him down the stairs and fall into his spot.

Without the light, he might have tripped over all the feral cats living down there with him. That's because his main hobby, job, and reason for getting out of bed, was drinking. He figured he'd achieved a master's degree in the bottle-tipping industry.

"My ladies, I'll be back before breakfast," he said to all the cats as he reached the propped-open door. Dwight opened it but didn't go outside. The light was funny, like it was morning. That would only be possible if he'd slept for a whole day. He was sure the last time he went out it was also morning.

He looked around for Poppy, hoping she could help him, but she wasn't in the alley. That made him even more anxious.

His life was a mixture of drunken stupors and periods of recovery, often in the city shelters near the wharf. Lately, he'd been going downhill, both figuratively and literally, since he lived in the sub-basement of a skyscraper.

"I did sleep all day," he said, curling his hand to block the bright sunshine sneaking into the alleyway from the east.

He wasn't greeted by honking taxis, which was a blessing.

Dwight scooted through the entryway, careful to ensure his door-propping brick stayed in place. If he had to get official help opening it back up, he'd have to pay the guy dearly.

It turned out he wasn't the only one using the side entrance. One of the security guards peddled drugs to some of his fellow panhandlers, though he was careful to avoid interacting with the guy, lest he try to hold his bed hostage, like last time.

"Let's see what suckers we can find today," he said to no one. San Francisco was a treasure trove of bleeding-heart residents and even more charitable tourists. He'd never gone hungry since he'd arrived from Seattle. The weather was better, too.

He came out of the alley, expecting to find the bustle of downtown San Francisco. What he found instead was silence.

There was absolutely nothing moving on the street. It was filled with cars, but they were parked at weird angles, like the drivers decided to get out and walk home. Except that wasn't it, either. The doors were all closed.

Nobody was out and about, not even his fellow travelers of the street. It was prime time morning rush hour. The streets should have been crawling with men and women holding their hand-drawn signs.

He looked down at his.

Lost job. Lost home. Won't lose faith. God bles.

He misspelled bless on a tip from a talkative tramp he'd met a long time ago.

They'll feel sorry for you if you misspell simple words. Works like a harm.

That got Dwight to respond, "You mean works like a charm?"

See! You interacted with me.

The man had been right. People did react well to his sign.

But today, there was no one to hassle.

Down the street, about six blocks away, a high-rise burned with thick orange flames engulfing the top ten stories. Below it, where there should be fire engines lined up for a mile, there was nothing going on.

"What did I miss?" he said dryly.

THREE

Fairfax, VA

Ted and Emily loaded the guns into the rear compartment of his four-door Jeep Wrangler. The blacked-out truck was his precious baby these days and he was proud to admit it. That was why he'd left it in the parking garage under his apartment, while he'd taken his beater pickup truck to Andrews when he flew out on Air Force Two.

"Okay, before we go, tell me what I'm forgetting," he requested of Emily. "We have guns, enough ammo to outfit a full platoon, water, a water purifier, a dozen ham sandwiches for on the road, and a backpack full of survival gear."

He didn't itemize for her, but he'd brought gear to help them if they needed to go camping, such as a tarp, fire starters, paracord, and the like. He'd also thrown in a bunch of cans of soup and vegetables, in case they needed real food.

Ted had also spent a few minutes changing his clothes. He'd put on jeans and a loose-fitting polo-shirt. He'd feel conspicuous walking around with two pistols holstered on his hip; the shirt helped cover them. He also picked up one of his little Ruger LCP pocket pistols and stuffed it in his front pocket. Just to be sure.

"It all looks good to me," she agreed with a shrug, obviously out of her element.

"Right," he said, looking her up and down in a wholly professional manner. "We need to find you some replacement clothes, ma'am. You aren't going to last long dressed like that."

Emily held out her arms as if she'd been dressed in rags. "What's wrong with my outfit?"

He smiled. "Nothing. You look very pretty. What I meant is that we need to both wear more practical and less conspicuous clothes."

She shook her head. "You can't tell the vice president she looks pretty. That's sexist."

"Are you serious?" he said with disbelief.

Emily smirked.

"Damn!" he added. "You got me again."

"It's too easy. And I accept your offer to change. Will you help me get into a neighbor's apartment to get some clothes?"

His unease showed.

"I authorize you, in my presumptive role as your commander-in-chief, to break and enter so that we may requisition clothing for our journey. I'll even leave a note telling them they can get reimbursed, just like you."

Once given permission, it made it a lot easier. He knew of a single woman who lived a few doors down who had a figure similar to Emily's. He used a crowbar to defeat the deadbolt and push inside.

"Dang, you really are prepared," Emily said as she followed him in.

He stopped in his tracks when he entered the living room. The television was on, though it only had a welcome screen for the television manufacturer. A large white towel sat on the leather couch, along with a hairbrush, a makeup bag, and a smartphone.

Ted walked over and picked up the phone, morbidly curious to see what it showed. "Oh, god," he exclaimed. The picture displayed the woman exactly as he remembered her. She smiled in a picture taken with a man who must have been her boyfriend.

He looked at the towel, assuming she'd gotten out of the shower to get ready for work. She probably liked to get herself ready in front of the morning news.

Emily had gone right to the woman's wardrobe, apparently without any of the second-guessing Ted suffered. About five minutes later, she came out wearing a loose pair of jeans and a low-cut black tank top. However, when she got into the room, she pulled on an airy long sleeve, button-down shirt. She also wore a pair of hiking boots. "Her clothes are a size too big, but they'll do. Good job."

"Yeah, glad to help," he replied from a mile away.

"Ted, you have to snap out of it. They're all gone."

He didn't think of himself as particularly deep or emotional, but he hadn't been right in the head since he saw those little soccer uniforms yesterday. As a military man, he had no conceptual trouble with the idea of dying for his country, but he could not square the mindset required to destroy children, and innocent women like his neighbor.

"You're right. I won't let this distraction happen again."

She took his hand and looked into his eyes with empathy. "Ted, I sincerely hope it does happen again. Hell, we need to allow the pain in. Both of us. But not yet. This is terrible to behold, no doubt about it. However, right now, I need you to help me get back to where I can do some good."

"I'm fine. Really. I think seeing this woman reminded me of my sister. She's gone."

"Maybe—"

"No, it's fine. I've come to terms with it. Everybody is dead on the East Coast."

"Not everyone," she reminded him. "Your niece made it."

"That's true," he said with renewed enthusiasm.

Emily seemed to sense the change in mood. She spun around in her new outfit. "So, you got what you wanted. I've changed my clothes. Can we go now?"

He now noticed she'd taken out her earrings and removed a thin bracelet. However, she'd transferred a small American flag pin from her other blouse.

"I thought you'd never ask." He smiled.

Since most everything was already loaded, they locked up his apartment door and then went down to the garage again. His Jeep started easily, and he pulled through the exit of the garage, happy there wasn't a gate or anything requiring a human to open it for them.

He centered his aviator glasses on the bridge of his nose. "Okay, ma'am. My plan is to get you to a radio, so I want to take you to the nearest Air Force installation. Well, Andrews is the closest, but we aren't going back there. We'll head north, to Pennsylvania. I've been to an Air National Guard post up there. I'm sure they'll have what we need."

Emily turned. At first, he imagined her dressed for a pleasant morning drive in the country. They even had the sandwiches for a picnic lunch. However, they weren't on a date, so he fought to dispel that illusion.

"Ted, are you sure we can't go south? That will put us closer to your niece."

"No, ma'am, though I appreciate the offer." As an uncle, he wanted to go down there straight away and make good on his promise to Rebecca. However, as a warrior, he knew that was foolish. "The JFK is going to make a hell of a target for the enemy. They aren't going to let it go, and the carrier isn't going to go out quietly. Assuming they're still in port, which I very much doubt, they certainly won't let us on board. They'd probably shoot first and never ask questions; that's what I'd do if I were in charge down there."

"I might think twice about promoting you," she said with mock fear.

"What I mean is you and I have a duty to get you safely to the nearest radio. Places like DC, Newport News, and Baltimore are all going to be hotspots for the enemy. If we stay on the backroads and keep our profile low, we can avoid detection until the cavalry arrives."

"When will that be?" she asked.

"I don't know," he replied. "But they'll get here sooner if we can talk to them. After that, assuming you're in good hands, I'll go for my niece."

Poor Sisters Convent, Oakville, MO

Tabby patted Donovan on the back as he slept. "Time to wake up."

"Mom, give me a few more minutes, all right? Dad gives me more, all the time." The boy rolled over and jammed his face in the pillow, but then slowly lifted it back up. His eyes grew wide when he saw it was Tabby standing over him. "What did I just say?"

"Nothing," she said while brushing it off. Audrey had thought she was her mom after the girl had passed out in the mine yesterday. Being mistaken for their parents was a weird phenomenon that made her feel important and helpless at the same time.

"Come on, guys," she said louder. "We have to get going."

Peter and Audrey sat up together. "What's the hurry?" Peter asked.

"I want to get on the road and catch up to the police. They must be close because the cordon can't be much bigger than the city of St. Louis. They could have never evacuated everyone."

She hoped to find someone in the big city. Someone who knew what the heck was going on, and, she was sorry to admit, who didn't blame the whole thing on God.

Sister Rose was a sweetheart for giving them a place to stay, and she was impressed with her wolf-dog, but Tabby wasn't ready to stop driving.

"I can offer you whatever food I have," Sister Rose remarked as Tabby and the teens put on shoes and gathered their weapons.

"I could eat!" Peter blabbed.

"No!" Tabby replied, feeling a little bit like a parent again. "We'll find something when we leave, okay? We have to get going."

Tabby pulled out the pistol she'd kept stuffed in her tight waistband. "Sister, will you take this gun? There could be bad people out there. You should be able to defend yourself. It's really easy—"

The nun put her hands out. "No. Please, I'm not interested in guns."

Peter tapped the tube of his shotgun. "Sister, you should listen to her. She's pretty smart. You may not need it for people, but you might for the..." He glanced uncertainly at Deogee, her dog. "Wildlife."

"God will care for me. Or he will not. A gun will not change my fate."

Tabby didn't think that was true, but she wasn't interested in arguing. It was better for her to keep the gun, anyway.

As Tabby gathered her stuff, she tried to figure out why she was so hot to get away from the religious woman. Was it because of what she'd said about missing the boat on God's calling? Were she and the kids left in God's dust? Or did it have more to do with the idea a supreme being could allow the murderous disaster to happen in the first place?

Tabby believed God existed, but her parents never made her go to church, so it didn't occur to her to pray for guidance.

"Thank you for everything, Sister. You saved our sanity last night." She looked at the kids. The two boys poked at each other like they were play fighting. "You saved my sanity, anyway," she said in a much quieter voice.

"You do have your hands full," Rose replied. "If you ever come back, please stay here. Deogee and I could use the company. We may be in for a long period of silence."

The wolf stopped and looked over when it heard its name.

"Sheesh, I hope not," Tabby replied. "I couldn't survive a day without chatting with someone."

Sister Rose became calm. "You would be surprised what you can do. I was a lot like you before I came to this place, at least in regard to the pressures of life, but I found solace and peace. I once spent a year of complete silence here."

"Didn't that drive you insane?" Audrey squealed. "I couldn't do that, like, for a single day."

Tabby was more impressed. "I couldn't do that, either. Why did you finally give it up? What changed?"

Rose seemed to chew on a response. "I gave it up when I saw the four of you."

Peter whistled.

"Wow. I'm honored. We all are." Tabby pointed to the teens, mostly because of the guilt she experienced for looking down on the woman. She was nothing if not filled with resolution. It was a skill Tabby needed to develop.

Rose held up her hand. "We all have our calling before God, and he does talk to us, but sometimes you have to know when he wants you to do something helpful for other people without his spelling it out. When you are out there with your shotguns and other implements of death, don't forget that."

Tabby saw that as her cue to leave. She took a moment to pet the dog, receiving gobs of drool for the effort. "Good pup," she remarked.

"All right, people. The tour is leaving. Next stop, downtown St. Louis, Missouri."

She didn't tell them she had no intention of stopping if things didn't get better. The cordon was out there, possibly growing larger every second they delayed. If she had to drive all the way to Canada to find her parents, she would.

The kids ran to the car like they were going to miss it.

She and Sister Rose hugged. "Good luck to you, Sister."

"And to you. I hope you find what you're looking for."

"I will."

FOUR

Poor Sisters Convent, Oakville, MO

Sister Rose watched the friendly young people drive away, and she had mixed feelings about letting them go. They all carried guns for one thing, which made her uneasy. But they were all so young. She believed it might have been irresponsible to let them go off on their own like they did.

"Come on, Deogee, let's go for a walk." Walking helped her think.

She wasn't ready to jump in a car and leave her home, nor did she have the ability to force them to stay with her. It would have led to conflict, which was an emotional state she'd worked for over a year to unlearn. Plus, Tabby had some hang-up about blaming everything on a gas attack. She'd tried to talk her out of that notion, but it was a lot like speaking to a stone wall.

"You lead," she said to the dog.

It was a relief to talk again and leaving the convent without being told by Abbess Mary Francis was similarly liberating.

The gray wolf dog paced in front of her as she left the yard and walked into the street, though the anxious female dog took a brief detour to revisit her dead master. The fallen clothes had blown into some bushes next to the sidewalk, making it difficult for the big girl to settle on one place to sniff, besides the yellow running shoes, which hadn't moved.

"Come on, pup."

They both moved away from the dead person. Rose was glad to let the dog search around but was also relieved it chose to be with her at all. Seeing Deogee around her old master made her worry she was about to be abandoned again. It would be a lot worse now that she'd sent those kids away. However, the dog continued to pace alongside her, even as they rounded a corner and went into a subdivision of new homes.

She'd barely gotten to look at the new structures go up, despite living across the street from the development. Her cloistered lifestyle gave her little time to stare out the window and reflect, which was how the new homes sprung up almost without her knowing about them.

Deogee's nails clicked on the hot pavement as they walked in the middle of the street. The smell of fresh lawns filled the air. Bird song and cricket chirps were the only sounds; there were none of the unnatural noises of life, like cars, garage doors, or lawnmowers.

The residential roadway went a little uphill. The trees in front of the homes were saplings, at best, which allowed her to see all the way to the end of the street a quarter of a mile away. As she expected, there were no people anywhere in sight.

"Hello?" she called out in a weak holler. "Is anyone here?"

No one answered. In fact, it seemed to get quieter.

"Hello!" she yelled in a stronger voice.

Deogee whined. Her ears were straight up, like she'd heard something up ahead.

"What is it?" she asked.

The furry ears seemed to search the air like little satellite dishes. When they locked on, she barked.

"What—" Rose began.

Another bark came from up ahead.

She hesitated, knowing another dog could lead to problems, but the gray wolf seemed intent on finding it. She'd gotten ahead of Rose and made it known she wanted her to follow. The dog looked over its shoulders, walked a few paces, then glanced back again.

Rose sighed. "All right, let's go look."

They didn't have to go more than a hundred yards. A black lab was inside the front window of a house a short way up the street. While they stood on the driveway, the lab barked endlessly from the front room. It constantly fought the drapes; they always wanted to hide the dog.

Rose rang the doorbell out of courtesy, though that drove the lab mad. The barking got a lot worse, making her wonder if she was doing the right thing by getting involved.

"She probably needs to be let outside," she remarked.

"They all do," she thought. That made her nervous. How many dogs were on this street? There were at least twenty houses. Each one could have a pet.

After jiggling the front door handle, she found it unlocked.

That made the lab go nuts inside, like she was about to invade its space, but it would be cruel to leave the dog locked up. Something had to be done.

She pushed the front door open, which released the black lab from its home. It wagged its tail furiously at her ankles, then it sniffed Deogee for a tense couple of seconds. Before Rose could reach it and give a scratch, the dog hopped off the front porch and did its business in the grass.

"We're here to rescue you, girl" she said, wondering if being with multiple dogs was going to be a blessing or a curse.

Leesburg, VA

"This is where you said the government bunker is located," Ted remarked as they passed the sign welcoming them to Leesburg. "Do you want to pop in and check it out?"

Emily thought about it for almost a minute.

"Emily?" he prodded.

"No, I don't believe we should. I've been thinking about what you said. If there's an unseen enemy out there, and if they drove into D.C. and were surveilling the White House, they will almost certainly have eyes on the one place all the politicians would go after a disaster. We should go through town while staying far away from any Best Buys."

"I'll do my best, but I don't know where the stores are located."

"Me either," she admitted.

"If someone's there," he added after some reflection, "we don't want to give them away. If I didn't know about it, maybe the bad guys don't know about it, either. It would suck if we brought attention to people hiding there."

"Good call. I'm behind you one hundred percent. Let's keep going."

Ted believed she'd made the right decision. It was too risky to poke around in places where they couldn't be certain there would be friendlies. The National Guard base in Harrisburg was a hundred miles away up Hwy 15; an easy morning drive. It was an obscure location with no military significance. If they had any hope of finding a working radio without being discovered, it would be there.

An hour into their drive, they passed a sign for the Gettysburg National Battlefield. "I guess that place is going to be forgotten," he said with regret. "Without Americans around to remember it, who will care what happened there?"

She spoke with grim firmness. "There will be Americans there again. This fight is far from over."

He glanced at Emily, proud of her for taking that stance. "I know, ma'am. I was thinking in the short term. The place should be filled with little kids learning about the big battles and bigger wars for their freedom. The visitor center movie might be playing right now, explaining things to an empty theatre."

He kept driving, realizing how big his part in this really was. His role in helping the vice president could one day be as talked about as General Lee forcing his men across those fields into murderous fire on the other side. It proved the point that even brilliant generals had bad days.

Ted couldn't afford this to be his bad day.

"Think," he willed himself.

Emily turned on the radio and went through the dial. It was the same story as yesterday: there was only one station still playing music. All the others were either gone, or they played 'station offline' automated messages.

"Why is this one still on?" she asked.

He shrugged. "Maybe they're the only one who thought to put a looped backup tape into the

51

rotation, in case of an emergency like this." He considered how he might have handled it. "We should listen for repeats."

"Why?" Emily asked.

He did a double-take over in her direction. "I don't know. I guess it would give us something to do, rather than worry about the fires, wrecks, and strange soldiers running around."

"Oh, right." She smiled.

They listened to the radio for many miles, sometimes suffering through terrible songs. As they got closer to Harrisburg, he expected the station to fade away like all FM stations eventually do when you get far enough from their transmitters, but it sounded as strong as it did back in DC.

The dial setting was the same as it was back home.

"100.0 on the FM dial," he remarked.

Amarillo, TX

Brent Whitman waved the men down the steps. "Put that stuff in Barney's cell. We'll use that as the storage place for all the cans of food. Toby's cell will be for water only."

He thought they'd put together a pretty good plan in a short period of time. Yesterday, after most of the prison residents fled to points unknown, six of the men had volunteered to stay with Brent in the lower level of the prison. Today, they focused on gathering supplies from the kitchen and infirmary. The only key he didn't give them was for the weapons locker inside the upstairs security booth.

"We'll keep the first aid supplies in the lower guard shack," he suggested.

The booth already had a small cabinet designed for medical supplies, such as bandages and aspirin, so it seemed to make sense.

"What, you don't trust us with the good stuff?" Paul, the gas thief, stood at the entrance to the cage with the water in it but pointed to the medical supplies in Brent's arms.

"I trust you," Brent laughed, "but tell me where you would go to fence this stuff?"

Paul was the shaggy-haired man who'd become the liaison for the remaining prisoners. He and Brent had always gotten along, and joked back and forth, but now Paul's jokes had an edge to them. It was probably because no one had a clue about what had killed everyone on the upper levels, or in the nearby towns. "I'm just kidding with you, Mr. Whitman."

"Please, call me Brent." He was secretly relieved. There was no reason to suspect the men would jump him, but any rise in tension could lead to that end. It was risky to even joke with them. "We're all equal down here."

"Is that why you have the fire stick?" Paul said, pointing to the gun on Brent's hip. The guy also liked to think of himself as a Native American. When he first came in, the man was deeply tanned, with unruly hair. He looked a little wild, like a native time forgot. However, as the months of his sentence wore on, he'd become a pasty white man, like the rest of them. Even the bird tattoos on his arms lost some of their outdoorsy charm.

There wasn't even a page in the corrections officer handbook dedicated to giving weapons to prisoners. No one ever thought it would be necessary.

Brent looked around the cell block to Paul and the five other guys. He'd known them all for months. "I'm an old man. Any one of you could jump me and take me down. You'd have already done it if that was your game. I have this gun in case we meet someone we don't know."

The phone rang on the security desk.

"Hallelujah! That might be Austin. The state government should have its act together by now." Brent kept the supplies in his arms and trotted to the security booth.

The other men followed at a distance.

He chucked the medical stuff on the counter, then picked up the desk phone.

"Hello?"

"Brent? Thank God it's you!"

"Trish?" he said with surprise.

"Yes! Is the prison open? Did the men get out?"

In a moment of clarity, he understood how the other guards intended for the prisoners to never see freedom. They'd fled the scene and had no intention of coming back. He'd done the same thing, to see the devastation with his own eyes, but he assured himself he'd always planned to return.

Maybe someday he'd ask her about it, but he decided not to hold that against her right then. "It's open, yes. I came back and you and the other guards were all gone. I figured everyone gave up. I... Well, I couldn't leave these men to die."

"Shit," she spit out. "I mean, I'm sorry, but look. I know where some of the men went, and you're not going to like it."

His high blood pressure went higher. "Where are they? Where are you?"

"I can give you two answers, but you'll only need one."

Prisoners weren't supposed to know where the guards lived, for their own protection, but if everyone was dead and gone, it wouldn't be hard to find the few living people left. Maybe they saw her lights on. Maybe she was out driving around.

Anyone could have broken into the police station to get addresses …

"Hell's bells," he drawled. "They're at your place."

"Yup."

FIVE

Harrisburg, PA

"There she is," Ted remarked from their position a short way on the bridge over the Susquehanna River. The town of Harrisburg was a bit to the north, but the far shore was mostly trees, so it was hard to see the buildings and streets of the mid-sized city from the highway.

The airport to the south was easy to spot, however, because it had been built alongside the river. The air traffic control tower stuck up above the low hangars and long runways right at the water's edge.

Even further down the river, the tall smokestacks of the Three Mile Island Nuclear Power plant peeked over the treetops. The drift of mist came out from two of the four cooling towers.

"It's too bad they couldn't let us drive right in," Emily complained, leaning against the side of the Jeep.

"Yeah, I'm trying to decide if we should drive north and find another bridge. I'd hate to ditch my Jeep." The flat, topless interstate bridge carried three lanes of abandoned vehicles in each direction, so there was no way to drive across. They'd gotten out to think it over.

"Well, the airport is right there. Maybe we walk across, get down to those railroad tracks, and sneak into the place? When we're done, we'll come back." She tapped the black Jeep on the door.

"I'm up for it if you are," he said, happy to know he didn't have to permanently abandon his rig and the supplies within.

"Tell me what I need, and let's get started."

He hustled to get what he believed was appropriate for a walk through hostile country.

"AR-15." He handed the gun over.

"Weapon's pouch." He gave her a small pouch she could sling around her waist. Inside, she'd have two hundred rounds of 5.56 caliber ammo. It was enough to be useful, but not so much she'd be uncomfortable.

"I'll carry the supply pack. I've got the water purifier, a water container, a little food, and some medical supplies. We should have enough stuff to stay overnight, too."

"You don't mess around," she said as if impressed.

They stepped off from the Jeep, but he turned around before he got more than twenty feet.

"What did you forget?" she asked.

"Nothing. It just feels like I won't see her again. Me and her go way back. I bought her the day my divorce papers went through."

She laughed. "You've been dating a car?"

He didn't know how to respond. Only a person who had escaped a bad marriage could understand what it meant to finally have something that was yours and only yours.

He chuckled, content to let things play out. "Yeah, I guess I have. You have no idea what kind of street cred this rock crawler got with me and my niece in the canyons of New York City. She'd make her mom sit in the back seat so she could wave at her friends from the front."

They started walking through the wreckage on the bridge.

"You were close with your sister?"

"Yeah. And Kyla was like a— Wait. She *is* like a daughter to me. Becca was the mom who never had her life together. I was the uncle who always came to straighten her out. Kyla was the good kid who somehow survived living with a single mother in that crazy city."

"Sounds like you had something to do with it."

"Yeah, a little."

"I'll be sure to find out where the JFK is located if we do make contact with anyone in the chain of command, okay?" Emily scooted around a large tractor trailer that had jackknifed on the bridge. It might have been there before the disappearances, because a couple of expired police flares were in front of it.

"It clears up once we get beyond this truck," he noted. "We're going to have to jog."

"Boy, you really want to make me sweat, don't you?" Emily laughed while simultaneously wiping sweat from her brow. It was morning in mid-June and the humidity over the river was probably at one hundred percent.

"That's my job," he said matter-of-factly. "But seriously, we'll be easy to spot in the open. I want to cross over as fast as possible." He considered going all the way back to the beginning of the bridge, then walking down the other span. It had cars from one end to the other. However, like most of his military calculations, that would take too much time with not enough benefit.

Emily searched the skies. "You think someone is watching us?"

He clicked his tongue against his teeth while thinking about it. "We have to assume someone is looking for stragglers like us. I'd rather be over there in solid tree cover." The shore upstream from the airport was dense with trees.

She pointed to the low concrete barrier alongside the edge of the bridge. "We could crouch down and crawl to the end. That would make us impossible to spot unless they were looking at the bridge from above."

He nodded. "Good thinking, but that will take ten times longer than running. Getting over and off the span will reduce our chance of a drone or other pair of eyes coming over us."

She shrugged. "That's why you're here: to tell me the correct way to do things."

"Ha! This is all-new terrain. I don't even know who the enemy is. It makes it really hard to know the correct way to do anything."

"Whatever. I jumped out of that plane knowing precisely what I was doing. Once I found you, and learned about the president, I lost my bearings. You and I are both doing this on a wing and a prayer." He appreciated the reference to their shared love of aviation.

"Amen," he replied.

They ran across the bridge, mindful the air was no longer friendly.

Saint Louis, MO

The car ride was quiet as Tabby drove them through the suburbs of south St. Louis, looking for anyone who might be able to help them. She'd found Sister Rose by chance, so there had to be others. One of them would know where to find the cordon blocking the rest of the people from the affected area of the disaster.

Naturally, it was Peter who broke the silence. "My grandma used to live up this way. I think her street might even be one of these around here."

He and Audrey sat in the back.

Donovan sat in the front, next to Tabby. He turned around. "Sorry she's dead, Peter."

"It's cool. She actually died before all this." Peter tapped his window, calling her attention to all the abandoned cars on the highway around them. "I only brought her up because she used to have a kick-ass house. I think they had a lot of money or something. She had the best televisions and audio equipment. I used to love going over there because I could watch whatever I wanted."

"Do you want to go there now?" Audrey asked with concern.

"No. Grandpa died before her. All her stuff is gone."

"It does bring up a good point," Donovan replied in his country-boy accent. "We should stop somewhere for food. Maybe a fast food restaurant was in the middle of cooking some burgers yesterday, and they're free for the taking now."

The city was a looter's dream, she realized. All of the grandmas could lose their big televisions if anyone came by with a big enough truck. And if she and the kids broke in somewhere and stole food, they'd be looters, too.

They already were, with the guns, but she tried to justify that as necessary for their security. She'd seen too many movies where the people died because they were unarmed. Not on her watch.

"Whoa!" she said. Up ahead, a pileup blocked a small bridge over a roadway.

"Go on the other side," Peter said from the back seat.

"No duh," Audrey laughed. "I think she can figure that out."

"I'm just trying to help," he replied.

It wasn't a simple thing because there was a concrete barrier in place of a median.

"We have to backtrack," she said as she slowed and prepared to turn around. "It's going to—"

A feeling came over her that she was being watched. It might have been someone in a nearby home next to the highway, or from inside one of the cars stacked up in the crash up ahead.

She hit the gas as soon as the car was pointed the wrong way on the highway.

"Whoa! Did anyone else feel ooky, like we're on camera?"

"No, but I wouldn't worry about it, even if someone's watching. We've got these babies." Peter patted his shotgun like it was a dog. He and Audrey had theirs stacked together between them. The butts were on the floorboard.

Tabby drove back a mile, or two, until she was able to go down a ramp, go under the highway, then go back up into the wrong lane of traffic.

Her tension built as she drove back to where the accident had taken place.

"Now I feel ooky," Donovan admitted. "From driving the wrong way like this. We could easily ram another car head-on."

She slowed to about forty miles an hour, partly to make Donovan feel better, but also so she could get a good look at the accident location. As she drove by, she searched for evidence someone was nearby with a camera.

The wreck had been caused when the cars spun out in all directions. The smaller cars had shifted lanes, but they got twisted with a school bus and a little moving van. She kept her eyes on the other side of the interstate as best she could but rolled on without seeing anything that looked like it didn't belong.

Audrey leaned forward and tapped Tabby on the shoulder. "You're really freaked out, aren't you?"

Tabby responded by turning halfway around. As she was about to address Audrey, motion caught her eye over by the wrecked bus.

"Holy—" She cut herself off.

"What?" Peter said, looking back.

"Did he see it?" she thought to herself.

What was it? It could have been a tree swaying in the wind. Or it could have been someone's clothes blowing up against the far windows of the bus. Or ...

Dad had used a four-prop drone to record footage from inside the mine during one of his publicity efforts. He'd hired a guy to drive the drone out over the lake and around the columns of rock. It was supposed to entice people to want to come to the mine and spend money to take a boat tour. She only remembered it as the time he had a helicopter underground.

The thing on the far side of the bus appeared to have the same general shape and white color as dad's camera drone.

She didn't look back. Whatever it was, she wanted to leave it far behind.

"The cordon has to be before downtown," she said with rising panic in her voice. It wouldn't be right to tell the kids about the drone because it would only make them nervous. And her even more nervous.

"Unless it wasn't a drone, you scaredy cat," she thought.

"The Arch!" Peter's excitement at seeing it cut through the tension with a verbal axe. "Let's check it out."

She rolled her eyes. "We aren't tourists. We're not stopping there."

Peter huffed. "We have to stop sometime, and I'm getting hungry. There are always people eating picnics and stuff. I bet we'd find something tender to eat, like Yogi Bear scoring a basket."

The Arch gleamed silver about five miles in the distance. If she stayed on the highway, which she planned to do, it would take them downtown and right by the monument.

"Well, actually, that might be a good idea," Tabby allowed. "If this town was under some sort of alert, they would almost certainly evacuate people to the most famous monument in the city. We might find people there."

Audrey clapped, then launched into a violent cough.

"Gas?" Tabby immediately thought.

She drove the car and waited for several tense moments as the young girl seemed unable to catch her breath.

"Does she need meds for her diabetes?" Tabby asked Peter, scanning the floorboards for the little cooler with her insulin inside.

Audrey shook her head and held up a finger signifying 'just a second.'

Tabby was worried sick something was wrong with the girl, and she'd begun to think about pulling over, even if there was someone watching. However, before she got too far down that path, Audrey cleared her throat.

"Sorry," she croaked. "I swallowed my gum."

"Unbelievable," Tabby let out with relief.

"I'm sorry," the girl replied. "I'm excited! I've never been to the Arch."

She and Peter hugged and pecked each other's lips. Donovan stomped his feet on the floorboards to celebrate.

Tabby rolled her eyes, though the kids couldn't see her do it. The world had come apart, and they were still thinking about tourism. But maybe that was for the best. If they thought too much about their lost friends and parents, they might never stop crying.

"Yay!" Tabby gushed to join in. "We're going to the Arch."

SIX

USS John F. Kennedy

After the drone made it over the horizon, the Marines went to the bridge to talk things over with Captain Van Nuys. Kyla followed but stood outside the hatch to listen. As a civilian, she didn't expect to be able to contribute and was content to stay out of the way.

The captain didn't even need to be told why they were there.

"The threat detection systems went offline an hour ago. We're driving blind right now. That's why that bird penetrated our airspace. I'm trying to find someone who can troubleshoot the software. Not long ago, we finally got the hangar lifts working, so I've sent my XO to get at least one F18 in the air to provide cover. But we have to do everything with a threadbare crew, so prepping the plane takes a lot of time. Assuming we can even find a qualified pilot to fly it."

Carthager replied with a salute. "Understood, sir. Where do you want us?"

"I want binoculars on every corner of the boat, plus up top." He pointed to the decks above the bridge. "Radio me if you see so much as a plastic bag floating on the wind. We can't let the enemy get that close again. They probably already figured out our weapons systems are offline, because the bird survived the overflight."

"We're on it, sir."

"Good. Dismissed." He paused for a second. "Miss Kyla, you can come in."

Her name startled her. How did he know she was listening in? Was she breaking the rules?

Carthager stormed out like he'd been ordered to eat barbed wire. He barely looked at her as she waited outside the hatch. A few others followed their leader.

When it was her turn, she went inside. The Navy man seemed to turn up his nose at

Meechum's uniform shirt on her, but he didn't make a further issue of it.

"How did you know I was there?" she asked.

"I saw you on the security cameras. At least those haven't been sabotaged."

"Sabotaged, sir?" She wanted to get beyond the fact she was loitering outside.

"You're a programmer, aren't you? Maybe you can figure out what's going on with the radar, sonar, phalanx canons, and everything else on this boat." He seemed frustrated and had likely been up all night.

"I'm sorry, sir, I only work on the nuclear containment routines. I wouldn't know the first thing about guns or radars." She didn't mention her off-duty hobbies, which included white-hat security intrusions. What some ill-informed people might call hacking.

"Damn. That's what the Navy gets for isolating each department in data silos. No one can cross over. Still, will you take a look at it?"

"I will, but can you tell me what's happened out there? Specifically, New York City. My mom's there and—"

The captain held up a hand. "Everyone is asking me that question. I'll tell you what I've told my sailors. We just don't know for certain who's alive. All indications are that the entire east coast is gone."

"Gone, sir?"

The older man's hard-charging eyes softened. "Look, we don't know anything for sure. Right now, I need your head here." He pointed to the computers.

"I'll try." She strode over to a terminal and took a seat. The computer had already been logged in. "These are your credentials, sir." Easy-to-find passwords were usually the first, and easiest, way to hack a system. He'd just broken a major Navy security rule.

"Didn't I tell you this is why they wanted me? I have access to all the subsystems. This is the only way you can access other parts of the ship. I need you to check the radar code. Tell me why it isn't online."

She tapped the keys tentatively as she tried to find some similarities to her own code. At first, there was no baseline; it was as if the subsystem was written by someone from a foreign country. Eventually, she did find a few common terms.

"I'm going to need a little time," she said distractedly, forgetting for a moment her boss was the captain.

"Take whatever you need but make it quick."

She glanced over, wondering if that was a mistake, or the way a captain normally spoke.

For the next hour or so, she plunged into the code for the radar array. She tried various avenues of approach to dig into the system, using her own experience in nuclear containment as a blueprint, but each time she thought progress was being made, she hit a dead end. Simple things had been complicated; on and off switches were now running with an 'if/then' loop, which was tied to other loops. There was no way to figure out the tangle without spending a lot more time.

Marines came in and out during her coding session. They reported possible sightings of aircraft and kept talking about Longbow 3 as if it was missing. She didn't dare ask about it, even though she was supremely curious.

"I've got it!" she blurted. The reason she couldn't make sense of the coding was obvious now that she knew how it was structured. All the back-end lines had been redone recently, and the comments denoting the most important changes were encrypted and written in a different language. She found the answer by accident, because the script writer had forgotten to encrypt one of them.

The captain rushed over. "You've figured it out? Do we have radar again?"

"No. Sorry. There's no radar, yet."

"Well?" He leaned in to see her screen. "Why not?"

"Sir, I can't fix this code because I don't speak Chinese."

Harrisburg, PA

The run across the interstate bridge left Ted and Emily winded. They'd hopped off, run down the embankment, and now caught their breath under a huge sycamore tree next to the river.

"This thing might act as an umbrella and keep us out of sight of any drones," Ted remarked.

"Is there something you're not telling me?" Emily taunted.

He took one huge breath, finally catching it. "What do you mean?"

"I mean... Are you protecting me from the truth about those drones? I've seen footage from overseas in the situation room. Drone operators can see in infrared, right? We're no safer under this tree than if we were walking around in the open."

"That's true of our drones. I have no idea of the capabilities of the people running the show out there. But I guess you're right. We need to assume they have at least what we do."

"And?" she needled.

He rubbed his sweaty neck in embarrassment. "And I guess I was protecting you. The truth is nowhere is safe from electronic surveillance technology. They can sense body heat, electronic signals, and they can tap into a smoke signal dialogue."

"Seriously?" she asked.

"I'm halfway kidding, but you get the point. That's why I wanted to run across the bridge. That's why I wanted to stay off the main highways. Our best and only defense is to stay away from high-traffic areas, and if we must use them, get in and out as fast as possible."

She shrugged. "Well, maybe it was nicer when I thought this tree could save us."

"Let's go," he suggested. "We've got a short run along this railway track, then we'll be at the Air National Guard facility."

They traveled for fifteen minutes, stopping once for a brief drink of bottled water. He'd brought the go-bag with their essential supplies, and she carried the ammo pouch, but otherwise they were traveling light. They jogged the tracks again as soon as they were done.

"This must have been a busy place," Emily suggested. "I've only been to Harrisburg a couple of times, and those were all in nice reception halls and school gymnasiums. The campaign trail didn't lead into railroad grades, like this one."

He admired her trotting confidently in the baking sun. She'd taken off her long-sleeve outer shirt and tied it around her waist, leaving only the black tank top. Still, she didn't seem to mind sweating and didn't complain at all until they'd almost gone past the entire property of the airport.

"Are we going to pass the whole thing?" She pointed to the right. The giant main terminal and air traffic control tower were behind them.

"Yes, this is our stop. It might surprise you to know this, but the National Guard base was shoved all the way down on the end, in those smaller buildings." He halted the forced march.

"Is that a funding joke?" she asked.

It was meant as a slight against her party, but the truth was both political parties seemed to enjoy reducing the expenditures for the military. He decided it wasn't going to do any good to complain, even as a joke.

"No, just a statement of fact. The place we want is on the end, out of the way. That's good for us. I didn't want to leave the safety of these tracks until we reached this side. Now we walk right in the back door."

The paved landing strips were on the far side of the row of buildings, so they wouldn't be seen by anyone watching those. He'd picked the path with the least chance of being detected, but the next part would require them to go out in the open.

"You ready to do some more running?" he asked.

Emily was undeterred. "I once ran a half-marathon for charity. I almost threw up, which would have made the news, but I got through it. I'm sure I can run across one little parking lot."

Ted chuckled. The long-term parking area between them and their destination was as big as a typical shopping mall lot. It was a mile long and half a mile wide. The orderly lot was filled with cars left by travelers before flying to their destinations.

"Stay close," he encouraged.

Once more, they ran into the open. Emily had it right by calling him out on being safe under the tree, but it did offer a minimal amount of safety. The truth about surveillance was they could be spotted from space when they ran out in the open.

If a satellite happened to be watching an obscure lot in Harrisburg.

San Francisco, CA

Dwight was in his mid-thirties, though people often mistook him for fifty. Life on the streets had been rough on him, though he accepted the trade-offs since he also believed it gave him the wisdom of a much older person, at least in respect for how to read the ebb and flow of the city.

Morning was a good time to hit up people near coffee stands.

Lunch was when he went down to the wharf area. Travelers gathered there to eat and line up for the afternoon tours of Alcatraz.

Dinnertime was when he mingled with tourists and locals on the streets around the restaurant district. After a nice meal, people were often in a good mood to give him a kingly tip.

But today, there was no ebb or flow.

Every car was abandoned. All the restaurants were empty. The wharf had no ferries coming or going, though one still floated in the bay like it was lost.

"Did the aliens come and get us, Poppy?" he wondered as he craned his neck to look at his shoulder. His colorful bird had found him after he'd left his sleeping quarters, like she always did. No one else ever saw it, try as he might to make them, but the bird always had plenty to say to him.

A shiny new Mercedes sat in the middle of the next street. The windows were open, like the owner had been enjoying the cool sea air on her drive through the city. A large designer purse sat all by its lonesome on the passenger seat.

Poppy didn't like him stealing from people, but it was sometimes necessary when days of rain kept away his normal clientele. He rationalized it as necessary to stay alive; plus, he always intended to pay back whatever he took. Someday.

This time, he left the big, juicy purse where it was.

He held up his hands. "I surrender! You can have the city! Take me to your ship!"

The fire burning in the upper floors of the nearby building created a dull roar in the background, and car alarms chimed endlessly far away, but all the normal city noises were gone. Especially laughter and talking.

"What, Poppy? Should I go to the stadium? That's a great idea." He paused as if listening to his friend. "What? No, I can't fly. How many times do I have to remind you?"

The stadium was miles away, through the heart of the city. He only went down there when he knew there'd be a baseball game; he preferred the sure bet of tourists at the wharf. He had no idea what day it was, and there was no one to ask, so he couldn't be sure if anything was happening there.

He glanced at the bird. "No, I don't have a phone to check the date. That's what normals do. Yes, I know everyone else has one; I'm much better than everyone else. I'm sorry to disappoint."

The pair argued back and forth incoherently for the next couple of minutes, and his voice got louder as their dispute amped up. Only after Dwight realized he was inside one of his famous "crazy scenes" did he put on the brakes and look around. "I don't think anyone saw us," he reasoned to her.

The crazy scenes always hurt his panhandling takes, so he tried to keep them at a minimum. Over the years, he'd realized the sometimes-nasty bird liked to instigate them. That's why she wasn't allowed to go into the basement where Dwight spent his nights. When the bird was around, it never shut up. Arguments ensued. He couldn't risk the loud racket calling in security and ruining the good thing he had going on. But, out in the open, he often had loud conversations with it. For some reason bystanders only heard his half...

"Yes, okay. I'll walk you down there."

Today, he didn't mind all the walking. Every new street brought the possibility of seeing someone new, and that would mean he could go back to his livelihood of panhandling. But once he got back into the skyscrapers of downtown, Poppy acted nervous.

"No, I'm not going back to bed, you don't have to worry. I'll worry for both of us because there aren't any people to talk to." He searched more places; in shops, the nearest bus stops, the street corners where normals always took pictures.

Poppy dive-bombed him with ideas.

Dwight shouted into the sky. "What? That's insane. You really think everyone is invisible? Including me? Including you?" He tried to wrap his mind around the statement, and what to do about it. However, Poppy really stepped up for him when she kept talking. She figured out a solution he assumed was ingenious.

"You sure about this?" he asked the bright-feathered bird while he strode over to where she wanted him. "Right here?"

The bird sang.

He sat inside a crosswalk at a normally busy intersection. Poppy's plan was to make it so he could see down four different streets to catch sight of invisible people driving their cars. He'd also feel them walking by, because they'd stay within the lines of the crosswalk. The regular people always did.

"You'd better be right," he said, "or I'm going to keep going to the stadium."

His bird said to be patient, and he always listened to his bird.

Dwight calmly waited to be knocked over by the invisible people. Then he would know he wasn't going nuts...

SEVEN

Harrisburg, PA

"I think these cars make it fifty degrees hotter," Emily remarked as they crossed the wide parking lot. After all their starts and stops today, it was already close to noon. There wasn't a cloud in the sky, and the sun was almost directly overhead.

"I can think of one thing we forgot when we left my house." Ted constantly thought about gear. What he could drop. What he forgot. Modifications to make it all better.

"An air conditioner?" she said in jest.

"A hat."

"Well, I hope you know," she panted, "I'm going to have to dock your pay for that. I'm keeping track of every mistake as part of the evaluation process for your job as my bodyguard."

He jogged to another row of cars, then stopped. When he looked back, Emily's face wore a look of concern. They needed to meet up.

"Come here," he pleaded.

"Did you hear that?" she whispered upon arrival.

He nodded affirmative. The faint whine of an airplane motor came out of the sky, but it was hard to tell from where.

She was going to say something, but he gestured for her to stay silent a little longer. The sound continued for a minute, but then faded. Finally, the world went back to silence.

"It's gone." Ted got up to look over the hoods of the two cars he'd jumped between. It all appeared the same as before.

"Any idea what it was?" she asked.

He'd been flying big four-engine jumbos for so long that he'd lost touch with his roots at smaller airfields like Harrisburg. It sounded like a single-prop civilian craft, but he couldn't say for sure.

By contrast, if any of a number of different jumbo jets had flown over, he'd be able to tell the make and model number of the airframes, and probably the type and model of the engines, too.

"For now, let's go with unknown. It sounded small, and possibly non-military, but I wouldn't bet our lives on it."

"Should we keep going?" She swept her arm across her forehead to clear the glistening sheen of sweat. It really was an inferno on the asphalt parking lot.

"We have to," he said dryly.

"That's what I thought. We're too close to turn around."

They smiled at each other for a second, then he got up and ran for the next row of cars. Emily followed a few seconds later.

He kept running after reaching the entrance to the lot. A ticket booth and gate had a few cars parked in front of them, as they were when the people inside disappeared, but he ran right by.

"Come on!" he called.

He'd been to the small Air National Guard facility a couple of times in his travels. It was basically a short row of one-story office buildings and a couple of small hangars. However, the main aircraft of the base were modified versions of the C-130 Hercules transport planes.

The sign above the main building said "193d Special Operations Squadron. Never seen, always heard."

"Jackpot," he said when he walked through the unlocked glass front doors.

"Thank God for air conditioning," she exclaimed when she got inside with him.

He was in a hurry, but he turned around to watch the small-framed woman approach. Her shirt was soaked with perspiration, and her hair was a mess, but she maintained her politician's smile.

"Yeah, power is still working here. I guess it pays to live next to a nuclear power plant, huh?" He led her into the facility, not sure what he was looking for.

"Doesn't it worry you? That the plant will blow up without human control? It melted down before, even with human oversight."

"That was decades ago. I'm sure they have safeguards in place for situations like this. Maybe the reactors shut down if no one touches a button for a few days. They have to plan for this, right?"

She shrugged. "I'm not an expert in nuclear power. Not even an amateur, really."

"Me either, but I do have some experience with this." He went through the door labeled 'Radio Room,' knowing he'd found what they'd come for.

The inside was filled with so much radio equipment, it forced him to stop and figure out what was what. Much of it was redundant, but he sifted through the amplifiers, repeaters, and equalizers to get to a desk with a common microphone.

"Here we go."

Ted went right to work shifting the dial to look for radio traffic. However, a few seconds after he began, he glanced at the chair next to him. A camo uniform lay uselessly on the seat, and some pants and boots were underneath.

"First, I'm going to listen," he advised Emily. "This radio can scan frequencies and tell us if there's anyone talking to the mainland from offshore. I would assume there is."

He adjusted the controls for a few minutes, sure he'd pick up some traffic.

"I'm not getting what I thought."

"Are you sure it's working?" she asked.

He rolled the chair back and forth by the nearby equipment, positive he'd notice if there was something turned off or otherwise squelching his signal, but it all looked normal. It should have been possible to hear something over the airwaves.

"This isn't what I—" Emily began.

He'd gone to civilian channels on the FM band to see if the radio was working. Sure enough, he heard an old rap song when he hit the right frequency.

"It's the same station we heard in your Jeep," she remarked.

They listened for a short time.

"I want to hear what happens when the song ends." He leaned back in the chair, content to rest for a few moments.

"You really wanted to hear this song, didn't you?"

He shook his head. "Rap isn't my thing. Old rap, even less so."

She rolled over a chair that didn't have any loose clothes in it. She sat down and slid up next to him. "Let me guess. You like music about pickup trucks, lost dogs, and cowboy-smitten women. Am I right?"

"Country? No. I do like rock from the seventies and eighties, though."

"Ah, classic rock."

"No, I call it plain old rock. Nothing classic about it. They broke the mold when the music industry went into the nineties. I haven't understood music since eighty-nine. Anyway, I—" The song came to an end. "Here we go."

A short series of beeps filled the air, but the playlist went into the next song.

"It sounded like a computer is running the DJ booth," Emily suggested.

"Yeah. Weird. I guess it really is on a digital loop. Nothing too exciting about it."

Absently, he thought the owner deserved an award.

'Last station on the air.'

St. Louis, MO

"This is the most confusing place I've ever been!" Tabby threw her hands in the air, despite being behind the wheel. "None of these streets go to the Arch. They go everywhere but there."

She'd parked in the middle of a wide avenue with wrecked cars all around her. The Gateway Arch gleamed bright in the morning sunshine from only a few blocks away, but it was seemingly impossible to find the road that went underneath it.

"Maybe we can try going on the highway again?" Donovan drawled from the navigator's seat.

The highway went into a channel below ground, cutting off the city from the park-like grounds of the monument next to the river. Being on the highway got them closer, but they wouldn't get close enough.

"Why don't you drive on the grass?" Audrey said as an offhand remark.

Tabby slowly turned to see her and Peter in the backseat. They'd each moved closer to their respective windows to try to help her navigate the confusing downtown streets. "You're a genius. Why am I trying to find roads and parking lots when I can drive into the park the old-fashioned way."

She got the car moving again and found the first cross street. It was one-way in the opposite direction, but she didn't pay attention to that. After going a couple of blocks, the roadway ended at a large church at the edge of the park. She drove onto a small parking lot, then continued onto a paved walking path lined with young trees.

"This is so much easier," Tabby crowed. "We don't have to follow the rules, because there are no police around to give us a ticket."

"We could give the Arch a lawn job," Peter giggled.

Audrey reached over and slapped him.

"Thank you," Tabby said to the girl.

As their tour guide, she couldn't lay a hand on them, but there was no stopping Audrey. She seemed to enjoy the role of riding herd on the unruly Peter. He seemed to like it, too. He laughed after she slapped him.

"I'm kidding!" he protested.

Tabby drove the path for about fifty yards, guiding the car to the top of a small rise. The Arch towered above like a sixty-story steel skyscraper. The other leg of the monument came down across a wide, flat field of grass. The open space was several football fields wide and long.

"What are those?" Donovan pointed ahead.

The field looked like it was being used as a staging area for a huge science fair. A long row of yellow bulldozers had been parked on the far side. Two more trundled along the tree-lined footpath on the other side of the most distant Arch leg.

Tabby stopped the car while still in the trees.

The middle of the field was dedicated to multiple models of flying drones. Those, she recognized right away. There were two rows of the smaller type her dad used for the mine, perhaps fifty in a line. Another row contained larger four-propeller drones, and they looked like they could carry cargo under their raised middles.

The closest row was a line of dozens of small, horse-like robots. Those were painted in camouflage colors, like kids had come by and glued fall leaves all over them.

"This doesn't feel right," Tabby said to herself. "Where are the survivors? The police? The fire department?"

"It's probably just the police." Donovan pointed into the air over the Mississippi River to their right. A normal helicopter flew above the mud-colored channel, then veered toward the far side.

"I don't know. This isn't what I expected." She still experienced unease about the floating drone she believed had been hiding behind that school bus. If it was being flown by the police, why hide at all? But what else could it be?

Tabby happened to turn to the left, toward the grass. A large bedspread had been tossed on the ground, and two sets of clothes, a man and woman's, were spread upon it. She looked away as soon as she figured out what it was.

"Go talk to them," Peter suggested. "We have guns, right? No matter who they are, they have to know something."

"I'll do it," Audrey added. Both kids in the back seat leaned forward, so they were almost between her and Donovan. Everyone but her seemed excited to see signs of people.

The two tractors weren't moving by themselves; living, breathing drivers were inside of each one. Still, the whole area didn't feel right. "Can we wait a second? I need to think this through, okay?" She smiled at the kids; hopeful she could suppress her own panic.

Donovan opened his door. "Don't worry, Audrey. I'll go check it out."

"No!" Tabby said at almost a scream.

Donovan flinched in fright.

"Please, don't go. We should all stick together." That was good tour guide protocol; something she re-learned when she got separated from her Dad and the main tour group before the disaster. "Stay in the car, please."

He'd managed to get one foot out the door, but he didn't hop all the way out. He looked ahead to the activity a hundred yards away, and she noticed her tummy roll back into a knot, as it had done down in the mine.

She had to try to keep them together. "I'll tell you what. I'm going to reverse back to the parking lot, then we can walk over to this hill and watch them for a while. If we see other survivors show up, we'll know we can safely enter, right? It will give us a chance to approach on our terms."

The sight of so many drones made her think of scientists lining up their equipment to survey damage after a disaster. If there'd been a huge gas leak or other calamity, it made sense they'd send in drones to make sure everything was all right before they'd send in more people.

Donovan closed his door. "We've got all day. Sure. Why not."

She put the car in reverse and backed away as fast as she dared.

The two tractors arrived under the Arch. She imagined them seeing her and sending over one of those drones to investigate what she was doing. Why was she here? How did she survive? Going even further into the world of panic, she imagined they might even kill them. Those horse-like machines didn't look friendly at all.

She'd nearly backed them all the way to the empty church parking lot.

"I think we're safe," she said. It took all her energy to keep from smashing the pedal to get away. It was good she kept a hold of that, however, because she probably would have crashed into the trees lining the walkway.

They were almost back at the lot when she saw movement in her rearview mirror.

"Uh oh," she gasped.

"What is—" Peter didn't finish.

A truck hit them from behind.

EIGHT

Poor Sisters Convent, Oakville, MO

Sister Rose checked the kitchen of the house, hoping to find food for the black lab, but the container of kibble only had five or six crumbs. The owners had let their supply dwindle to nothing. Now it was her problem.

"I guess people disappeared on dog-food restocking day."

She was able to fill the water dish labeled 'Biscuit.'

As soon as the black lab did her business, Sister Rose encouraged her to go inside again, but all she wanted to do was play with Deogee. The pair rolled around on the front lawn, growling and barking, making her worry they were going to kill each other. However, each time it looked like blood was about to spurt out from a neck, the dogs got up and started it all again.

She finally took a seat on the front porch, content to watch the dogs play. It gave her a chance to think about what had been going through her head since she'd let the lab outside.

"What am I going to do with you, Miss Biscuit?"

She wanted to get the dog back inside her house. That would restore things to the status quo, and it would give her time to think and pray on it.

While she contemplated the fate of one dog, she realized other dogs were further up the block. The faint echo of barking resonated from that direction, probably because they heard the playful barks of the two in front of her. How many of those were hungry? How many owners would have left food for their pets?

Rose figured she could buy food in bulk at the pet store, then bring all the dogs into one big yard to feed them. She could get the communal van, leave an IOU at the store register, then load the bags and bring them back. As she worked through the logistics, it seemed insane.

"God, is this my burden to carry? I now have to care for every dog I find?" Her terms of acceptance into the convent never said anything about animals. She'd fallen into taking care of Deogee, and she wouldn't turn a blind eye to this lab, but she believed her calling was to take care of people, not animals.

Rose looked down the residential street toward the main road. Tabby and the young children were now somewhere out there.

"I shouldn't have let them out of my sight."

Was it another failure of hers? Was God telling her to go with them, but she'd refused to listen? She exhaled in frustration. Nothing made a bit of sense anymore.

Deogee surprised her with a lick on her cheek.

"Oh, are you done playing?" The lab sprawled out on the grass, panting like a little engine. "You wore the other one out completely."

Her gray-furred wolf-dog sat next to her, as if to silently answer her question.

She humanized the dog by talking for her. "Yeah, mom, Biscuit couldn't keep up with me. Can we find some more friends?"

She laughed at imagining her speak, but the word "mom" surprised her. It was a word she'd given up when she'd put on the nun's habit. It hadn't even crossed her mind the entire time she'd been among the other sisters, because she'd found the life for her. Total devotion to God. However, just saying the word, and being responsible for the gray wolf-dog, made her see life a bit differently.

Rose still wasn't sure what it meant, but as she continued to think about it, a buzzing sound came from somewhere over the houses. Deogee got excited when it grew louder, probably because Rose did as well.

"We might finally have some help," she suggested.

The sound was hard to pin down, but it was definitely not natural. She likened it to a small airplane propeller.

"Here, puppy. Come here." She patted her knees at the front door to get the black lab to come in the house again.

Rose popped inside the elegant front living room. A patch of dried yellow stained the carpet, suggesting the canine did her business on the floor while unsupervised. Her owner had been there yesterday; the familiar tangle of clothing was on the carpet. It looked like the dog had been nosing through them...

"Inside!" she ordered, hopeful she could figure out a command it would recognize.

Deogee paced back and forth, as if trying to interpret her words.

She stepped further inside. "Biscuit! Come!"

Deogee came right in, but the black lab was still lying on her side in the grass.

The wolf watched her intently for a few moments, then ran outside again. Its long claws ticked off the hardwood floor of the McMansion-style home.

"Come!" she repeated.

Deogee got the other hound to its feet and led her through the doorway.

"Good pups!" she cheered. Her dog was smart.

She closed the door as soon as they were in, but then cracked it open again. The whiny engine sound seemed to come from down the street, nearer to her convent. Perhaps someone was looking over the place to confirm there was no one left alive.

If she'd been down there ...

She glanced over to the dogs; they were roughhousing again. This time, they did it on the family room's wooden floors. They got tangled in more clothing, kicked over a plant stand, and jumped on and off the fancy couch.

"What do I do?"

Harrisburg, PA

It was hard to know the name of the last radio station on the air because neither of them was familiar with radio in Harrisburg's listening area. It was made worse because the music channel

107

never gave out its call sign. It never ran a commercial or other break.

"Just like when we heard it in the Jeep. It looks like it is right at 100.0 megahertz on the FM band, though I don't know how the FCC let them license that. All civilian radio stations are supposed to end in odd numbers. 99.9 and 100.1 were probably taken over by this superstation. In DC, they call it Super One Hundred, or something like that. No idea what they call it here."

"I should probably know how they licensed it," she suggested, "but I think they started up before I came to office."

"Don't worry about it, let's just find the local station. I suppose we could look in the phone book for Harrisburg and track it down that way. Then we could go pay them a visit to see if someone's there."

"I'll look for the book," she replied.

Ted scanned other stations for about ten minutes while she searched. He didn't have a frequency guide in front of him, but he did know some shortwave aviation frequency bands. That let him listen in to air traffic flying over Iceland and Great Britain, but he couldn't hear anything over the Atlantic closer to America, which should have been bustling with traffic for planes coming back to the mainland. "I'm at a loss," he admitted.

Emily heard him from across the room. "About what?"

"I can hear traffic out there, but it's all far away. I thought for sure we'd hear some flights coming across today."

He scanned more frequencies until a voice came through loud and clear.

"Bingo," he said to himself.

"What's that?"

"This is an old Navy HF high command frequency. I didn't think it was used anymore, but they're broadcasting."

"A what and a what?" she chuckled, moving back over to him.

"Listen," he advised.

'...repeating: By order of General Preston Worthington, Supreme Allied Commander of NATO, and acting leader of all armed forces and civilians of the United States. All United States military units in Europe have been placed on hold until damage assessment from terrorist attack are complete. All US Naval vessels, aircraft, and personnel are to avoid continental US airspace at this time. Threat of second attack deemed likely. Repeating...'

"Ted?" Emily said with worry steeped in her voice.

"That explains why there is no allied forces here, even after a day," he remarked. If there were no US military units coming to their rescue, it changed this whole game plan, especially regarding the nuclear briefcase. Maybe it would be worth finding the JFK. It was the only friendly unit he could be sure was still nearby. That was how they could get a message up the chain of command.

"Ted!" Emily shouted.

"Yes?" he said, giving her his full attention.

"There's something coming across the bridge." She pointed out the window, across the airfield and toward the bridge where he'd parked his Jeep.

He ran over to get a better view. They were a couple of miles down the river from the bridge, but the large military wrecker was easy to see as it shoved cars aside with its giant blade.

"My Jeep!" he said with despair as he realized it was part of that clearance project. All his precious supplies fell, with the Jeep, into the river below.

She tapped his arm. "What do we do?"

He looked back and forth between the arriving convoy and the radio. It was too large to take with them, and there wasn't enough time to trawl through the long list of frequencies where he might learn more information about the worldwide situation. Could he get a call out to someone? Should he?

"We can't stay here," he said matter-of-factly. "We can't worry about the radio station, either. Help might not be coming like we thought."

The VP pointed to the microphone. "But we should call out for help, right? Tell them we're alive. Americans are alive here on the mainland."

He clicked his tongue on his teeth to think. "I don't think we should, Emily. The general just said US forces are not anywhere close. If we give ourselves away, the bad guys might come looking for you. For us."

She seemed like she wanted to dispute him, but her face softened in resignation. "We should go, then. Right?"

He looked at the airfield. A couple of large C-130s sat on a remote part of the tarmac. Those were laden with antennas as part of the mission of the 193d squadron. But there was also another, smaller, plane on the field.

"Ted? We should be leaving..."

"I know. I'm thinking of doing something risky." The safe play was to run off through the giant parking lot. They could find an abandoned car and blend back into the countryside. The problem with that plan was that there was nowhere to go out there. He wanted to get further to the east—closer to friendly forces who would eventually get the clearance to come in from England—before the enemy secured the area in and around DC. If they were already here in Harrisburg, they were spreading out faster than he'd given them credit. He pointed where he wanted her to go.

She turned to look. "You've got to be kidding."

Amarillo, TX

Brent had barely made it twelve hours before he was faced with a life-or-death choice. Trish's emergency call reminded him of his journey yesterday to the nearby towns. There wasn't just no one there, but there was no law there either. Trish and the other guards had gone out into an apocalyptic version of America where police officers wouldn't respond to any 911 calls.

Her cry for help fell squarely on his shoulders, unless he could come up with a miracle.

He'd called everyone he could, yesterday, but he figured he might have better luck today. After all, if he'd come back to work, maybe others did, too. Brent scrambled for the phone book and leafed through to the number for the Amarillo PD.

"Pick the hell up," he ordered through the phone.

It rang for twenty seconds before he slammed the handset down. He might have had better luck with some of the small jurisdictions around Amarillo, but even if they picked up, they wouldn't be likely to drive all the way up to the prison, then go even further to reach Trish's trailer park.

The six orange-suited prisoners had congregated outside the open door of the security booth. For the twentieth time, he acknowledged how easy it would be for them to bum rush him in the small chamber, take his gun, and then...

He shook his head to clear his brain. There was no time for second-guessing.

"What's up, boss?" Paul asked from the doorway.

Brent chewed on his bottom lip, worried that he'd regret what he was going to do next.

"Come with me, guys," he said, jetting out of the booth.

The six men followed him up the steps and down the main level concourse. He'd closed the bars for the hallway to the administrative offices, but now he opened them.

He spoke again once he got into the warden's wing. "Yesterday, I went home, not sure what I was going to do without my friends. You get to be my age and friends are hard to come by. They die off at an alarming rate, and I'm talking about even before this disaster struck."

Brent pulled out a glob of keys and found the one he needed.

"Anyway, I came back because I realized at least one of my friends was still alive. She was sweet, sassy, and tough as nuts when the manure spanked the fan."

"Aw, thanks, boss," one of the men at the back joked.

"No, you dumbass," Paul replied. "He's talking about Ms. Trish." He turned to Brent. "You have the hots for her?"

Brent laughed. Maybe if he'd had a billion dollars, she'd find him attractive for his money, but he was about forty years older than her. In this part of Texas, that made him like a grandfather to her. And, if he was honest with himself, he thought of her more like a daughter than someone he had the hots for.

"No, I didn't," he said dryly. "But some of the prisoners I let go last night must have an interest in her."

He went into the nondescript office next to the warden's. The lights were off, and there were no windows, so he had to flick on the switch. He continued to a second door on the back wall.

"Who?" one of the men behind him asked.

"I don't know. Maybe I should have asked her, but it didn't matter to me. I made a mistake not telling Trish and the other guards I was opening the cells. She shouldn't have to suffer for it."

He hurriedly unlocked the next door but stepped in front of it before opening it. "You guys are small-time criminals. I never did hold that against you, and I tried to be neighborly in our day-to-day so you wouldn't become worse men for having been here. I always thought of minimum security as a second chance for guys like you. But once I open this door, your second chance is going to directly impact me and my young friend. I hope you'll take this trust and give it back to me by doing one small favor."

"What do you want, boss?" Paul the hippy-haired man asked with great interest.

Brent swung open the door to reveal the armory.

"I want you to help me rescue Trish."

NINE

Harrisburg, PA

"Ted, you know I trust you, but are you sure about this?" Emily followed him outside the Air National Guard offices, but he stopped at some tall shrubs at the edge of the tarmac.

"I think so." He caught his breath for a second and steeled himself for the next part. "Yes. If we can get to that plane, we can head east faster than any other mode of transportation."

"But won't they see us? Isn't that why we couldn't use the radio?"

He shook his head and pointed to the bridge upstream. "That's why we're waiting for them to get across. You and I went right for the railroad tracks, which got us here in the most direct route. They'll have to take surface streets, which should keep the bulk of the airport between us and them." He ran his fingers through his hair while thinking of every possibility he could. "I don't know. It's a risk, but maybe they won't see us take off."

Emily cinched the shirt tied around her waist, like she was ready to do as he asked. Together, they watched the big plow clear the rest of the bridge, then drive over the near side, which was free of cars. Five or six Humvees followed behind.

The second they all made it across the bridge and went behind the tree canopy, he tapped her on the shoulder, then pointed to the plane. "Run!"

He was drenched in sweat again by the time he reached the little Cessna 172. It had come to a stop out in the middle of the taxiway and he took a chance that meant the pilot was either heading in or out when the attack happened. After wiping the sweat from his eyes, he peered inside.

"Yes!" he huffed. "They're in there." Ted thought about how that sounded. "Well, what I mean is we have a chance now."

Emily patted him on the shoulder. "It's all right. I know what you meant. The clothes are just clothes now. Not people."

He opened the door. Two sets of outfits were on the front seats, including two large pairs of headphones with attached mics. More importantly, the key was already in the ignition.

"I'm sorry," he said as he pulled the clothes out and threw them on the ground. "Get in," he said to her. He shoved their equipment in the back compartment.

While she ran around the front, he hopped in and got settled. He could skip almost all the pre-flight checks because the plane was already operational, or it wouldn't have been where it was. He set the fuel mixture and throttle where he wanted them, then waited for Emily to climb in.

"This is like being in your Jeep," she commented as she put on her seat belt.

"A little," he agreed. "A bit cozier."

He glanced up front to check for anyone walking nearby. When Emily saw what he was doing, she tipped open her window and yelled, "Clear prop!"

They shared a look.

She winked. "I've been flying since I was a kid, remember?"

"How could I forget?"

After he turned the key, the plane's propeller sparked to life. The sound level was loud, but not obnoxious.

"Here, did you see this?" He handed the headphones to her. Once on, he added, "Can you hear me?"

"Check," she replied.

Ted did a cursory inspection of oil pressure, fuel level, and avionics, but he left the transponder off. That was a no-no back when things were normal, but now he planned to fly off the grid. No need to broadcast their flight plan to a dangerous world.

The 172 was the plane model he'd learned to fly decades ago. It was one of the most common aircraft in the world, and flying it was rudimentary compared to the jumbo airframes he'd been tossing around. He had the plane taxiing toward the runway in moments.

"We're flying with visual flight rules today," he said in a cheery voice. He didn't want Emily to know how worried he was that they'd be seen.

"There's no one in the tower to clear us anyway," she added.

He glanced back to the tower as second-nature and caught sight of movement at the end of the runway. "Dammit! They're already here! They must have gone off road to get down the railroad grade like we did." They had four-wheel drive trucks; he should have anticipated they'd disobey traffic rules.

"Go, go, go!" she insisted.

He was faced with another dilemma. They were at the end of the commercial runway, which was probably 10,000 feet long. If they took off toward the trucks, and they shot at them, they might end up in a fiery wreck like Airforce Two.

Emily seemed to notice the problem immediately. "We have to take off downriver."

She pointed left, which was also the ending of the strip.

Ted hit the throttle and headed out onto the runway.

"I think they've spotted us." He pointed to the trucks through the front glass. Two of them drove toward the buildings, but three others turned to get on the runway, as if intending to block their departure. The Humvees sped down the strip side by side to cover the most ground.

"There won't be enough space," she said sensibly.

Ted continued to taxi as fast as he dared right toward the trucks.

"Oh, Ted, you're giving me a heart attack."

He expected gunfire to come barreling at them, but so far, the trucks seemed content to speed their way. Maybe the guys inside wanted to make sure he and Emily were the bad guys before killing them?

Ted went as far down the runway as he dared, then jammed on the brakes and turned them around. There was no rearview mirror, but he guessed the trucks were a couple thousand feet

123

behind them. Well within rifle range if they wanted to hit the giant metal target.

"Here we go!" He adjusted the fuel mixture, and for one stomach-clenching moment, the engine bogged and threatened to stop, but it got stronger a moment later. He gave it more throttle and held the yolk as they started down the short section of runway.

Emily held her lap belt as if frozen with fear.

"How do we look over there?" he asked, simply as a way to make her feel useful.

She looked out her window. "Clear to the end."

The Cessna was probably as old as he was—they'd been making nearly the same model since the 1950s—but the engine sounded strong, and he gave it as much throttle as he thought it could take.

"We're well inside the thousand-foot threshold," she advised.

"With a slight headwind," he countered. He guessed they had five-hundred feet until the end of the paved runway. Beyond that, there were a few navigation lights, then the river. "I'll tell you when it's safe to get up and move about the cabin," he mused.

It was always important to keep the passengers happy.

A "pling" sound made him and Emily look at each other.

"Was that a gunshot?" she asked.

St. Louis, MO

"Oh my god!" Tabby blurted out. "Someone hit us!" Her heart had stopped beating for a few seconds, but now it came rushing back like a tidal wave. Her breathing became erratic as she fought the panic.

"Quick! Get the guns!"

The truck struck them in the rear, but they'd been moving slow, so no one inside her car got hurt. However, the three kids seemed as jittery as her.

She gripped her shotgun, fought to get her seatbelt off, then opened the door. Belatedly, she put her foot on the emergency brake to keep it from moving.

The four of them spilled out of their respective doors, guns at various states of readiness.

Peter was behind Tabby, and he had his gun raised at the two men in the white truck. Audrey's shotgun slid out the door when she opened it, and she cussed at herself for letting it drop to the cement.

"Come out!" Tabby yelled to the other occupants when she finally got herself together.

As she stood there with her shotgun, she wondered why holding the gun was her first thought after the crash. Shouldn't she be getting out insurance information?

The driver put up his hands and spoke out the open window. "Don't shoot." All she could see was his face, because he sat high up in the truck. However, it was covered in dirt, like he'd spent a lot of time working on cars in a garage. His white and gray mustache was stained with dirt, too.

The passenger was younger and not as dirty. He put his hands up like his friend.

She strode past Peter and put some space between her and the driver, but she wanted to get a better look at him and his truck. The giant vehicle had a large cylinder in the back, as if it was used to deliver water. It said MSD, with a picture of the Arch on it.

"We don't want to mess with your operation," she advised. "All we want to do is find the cordon."

The older guy laughed. "You think we're with them?"

She pointed at the Arch symbol.

"We're with the Metropolitan Sewer District. M-S-D."

"Oh," she breathed out, feeling a tiny bit better.

The man went on. "We've been watching the Arch since this morning. Hoping we'd see some people who weren't playing with computer toys."

"So, you really aren't with them?" Peter pressed.

"Nope."

"Who are they?" Tabby wondered aloud, lowering her shotgun a bit.

"No idea, but they are the only people we've seen in the city since we came out of our job site yesterday. We spent a free night up in the Riverside Hotel, but it wasn't as fun as you'd think. It was like we were in a haunted city. The lights were on, but nobody was home."

That described her experience to a T. Driving into St. Louis was like going into a cemetery. She should have been overjoyed to see signs of life under the Arch, but now she felt better about doubting the whole thing. Here was someone else expressing the same misgivings.

Tabby finally pointed the shotgun at the ground. "We're sorry for the guns. I think we're all scared out of our minds."

"I'm not," Peter bragged as he patted the pistol in his police belt. He lowered his shotgun, though.

She pointed back down the path. "We should get out of here. They have tractors and drones and all kinds of weird...things...that could come get us."

"That's what we saw from up there." He pointed to the round hotel at the edge of the

Arch property. "We came down here to stop you from going in, but we didn't expect you to drive on the path." The guy chuckled. "I'm Gus, by the way. My partner here is Vinny."

"Hey," the other guy said. She could barely see him from her perspective on foot.

"Agreed on leaving," Gus said matter-of-factly. "Why don't you follow us? I'll take us into the city where we can talk."

"No way!" Peter burst out.

"Wait," Tabby said in a more measured tone. "We'll get back in our car and follow you, but don't try to lead us to those people." She thumbed in the direction of the Arch.

Gus smiled, though he was missing a couple of his teeth, making him look like a hobo who had happened upon the truck, rather than an employee of the company.

"Donovan, guys, let's get back in." Tabby ushered them inside the car like a sheepdog with a wild flock.

Peter seemed to resist. He kept his shotgun at the ready and took small steps in reverse, like the two men were going to get the drop on him. Eventually, however, he jumped in the backseat.

Tabby got in a few seconds later.

After setting the gun on the floor between her and Donovan, she took a few seconds to let the fear shake out of her. They'd found more people who'd survived the disaster, but it didn't instill nearly the same confidence as when they'd happened upon Sister Rose and her dog.

"I don't trust them," Peter said the second all the doors were closed.

"I don't, either," she agreed. "But we need to find out what they know. Maybe they'll tell us where we can go to get safe. Someone has to know."

The MSD truck pulled off the lot.

After a second of deliberation, she decided to follow.

TEN

USS John F. Kennedy

After confirming Kyla couldn't help with coding and notation done in a different language, the captain sent her off the bridge. She and Meechum went back to their target shooting, but the range took on a more ominous feeling for Kyla because it had the potential to become an active battlefield at any minute. They both kept one eye on the target and one on the sky.

The other Marines took watch at both ends of the super carrier, acting as simple lookouts for the billion-dollar war machine.

"Do you think they'll come back?" she asked when she couldn't take it anymore. Meechum and the other Marines never seemed to worry about anything, which made it more frustrating for her. She worried endlessly about what might be out there.

"If they do, we'll be ready. We're topped off on ammo and have more than enough to kick anyone off the boat we don't like."

Kyla shook her head. "I wish I had that kind of confidence."

"You can," the short-haired woman replied as they both stuffed rounds into their pistol magazines. "You just have to believe."

"That sounds like Peter Pan, not someone like you."

Meechum turned. "What do I seem like?"

Kyla laughed. "You're the most intense woman I've ever met. How you hang with those tough guys I'll never know. I want to be like you, but the most dangerous thing I've ever done, before yesterday, was a weekend hike on part of the Appalachian trail when I was in high school. And that was with a big group of people."

"Attitude, my young friend. The secret is to always act like you know what you're doing. It's something boys learn when they're young, though I can't understand how. Any problem these guys get, they jump in, grab it by the short hairs, and figure it out. You and me? We've been taught to stop and think things through. Be careful. Always look before you leap."

"Yep. Those last bits sound like me," Kyla chuckled.

"Well, unlearn all that garbage." Meechum pointed to Kyla's pistol. "When you're in your bunk room tonight, take it apart. Learn the pieces. Put it back together. Then, do it again. It isn't that hard. Get it done."

Meechum held up her own pistol. "When you master this, do the same for heavier stuff. Eventually, you can break down a sniper rifle in your sleep. That will earn you some points with the men." She pointed at one of the Marines standing guard nearby.

"I don't really care, but have you ever gone out with one of them?"

Meechum's face lit up with a "girl, let me tell you" look, but it changed again when she pointed toward the coast. "Incoming!"

Kyla had the foresight to grab an extra magazine for her pistol, then she ran with

Meechum toward the island of the aircraft carrier. The other Marines on deck stayed where they were; already heavily armed.

"Hang out here," Meechum advised. "Let's see what we've got. It's a chopper, for sure."

"Not a drone?" Kyla wondered.

They waited for a minute or two before Meechum seemed ready to give her an answer. "No alarms have gone off, so it's one of ours. Longbow 3, I'm pretty sure." Despite her haughty attitude, the woman was clearly glad it wasn't an enemy.

"Follow me," Meechum ordered.

Kyla didn't want to go out on the deck, but the helicopter swooped in and landed about a hundred and fifty yards away. Meechum had her stick to her like glue.

"Do we have to go so close?" Kyla remarked, though Meechum didn't hear her. They continued to inch closer, until they were about fifty yards from the spinning blades of the large helicopter.

"This Seahawk took a scout team out this morning," Meechum yelled. "These are our people!"

When the aircraft had settled on the deck, the rear doors opened. Kyla recognized the two men in the back. They were from Carthager's squad.

They hopped out and went over to Meechum like she was a customs official.

The first guy yelled like a lion; Kyla heard him even with the wash of rotors. "We didn't find jack squat! I hope you have better luck!"

He patted Meechum on the shoulder, then he and the other Marine went by. They barely looked at Kyla as they headed away.

Meechum glanced at her, then leaned in so they could chat. "The captain said two people have to go these recon missions; one for each side. Carthager also said you have to earn your keep, so how about it?"

Kyla recoiled in horror. "Not me! I'm just a..." Meechum was a Marine. Kyla was a civilian. That seemed like enough of a liability to get her a pass from this duty, but the salty Marine didn't seem to be in the mood for lame excuses. "I'm just not equipped to go with you."

Meechum pointed to Kyla's pistol. "You've been training all morning. No one is going to screw with you and your weapon. If they do, just screw with them back."

It was the kind of thing a no-bullshit Marine like Meechum would say. Not Kyla the programmer. But she figured out the other woman was trying to help her overcome her confidence issues, so Kyla wasn't going to disappoint. "I'll follow your lead."

"That's my dudette!"

Harrisburg, PA

Before Ted had a chance to worry about possibly getting hit by gunfire, the plane made it to the end of the runway.

"Come on!" he yelled at the struggling engine.

The Cessna 172 was a small plane with tricycle-style landing gear. The three wheels were always down, so when he pulled on the yolk to get the old craft into the proper upslope, he worried he'd hit the navigation lights and lose the tires.

"A little more," he said, mostly to himself.

The plane caught an updraft the instant before hitting the lights at the edge of the field, and Ted used every last inch. However, rather than build on that success and keep going higher, he let the 172 fly at treetop level until he was out over the water. Then he dipped back down.

"Ted, my mom was the stunt pilot. You're making me regret this mode of transportation."

He settled the plane about ten feet over the Susquehanna River and stayed close to the left shore so the trees would hide them temporarily from the men at the airport.

"I'm sorry. We barely had enough runway to get in the air. That was a near-run thing." He had survived fighter-pilot levels of g-force training, but he'd never come as close to losing his lunch. "And I think we got hit by at least one round."

She looked out her window. The wing was above them, so she could easily see if there were any holes in the underside. He scanned the wing above his window, but only for a moment.

"The river doglegs right, to the south. We'll be visible to them for a minute or so until we get farther down the river. Hang on."

He angled the nose up and rose to about fifty feet.

Emily looked out her window to the rear. "I see them back there."

"Are they shooting?"

"I don't think so. One of the trucks is going to the base, though. Another is sitting at this end of the runway, like it's watching us leave."

"Damn. This is all happening faster than I thought. They're spreading out from airport to airport, like we'd talked about."

The Cessna was up to speed now, so his maneuvering was more fluid as he rode above the treetops heading south. Emily saw the airstrip, which meant they saw them back. That gave him a few extra seconds to worry about getting shot.

"Almost clear..." he said in an even voice.

"I don't see it anymore," she replied. "Wait!" Emily paused for two seconds. "No, now it's gone for good. We have an island between us and them. There's plenty of trees blocking us."

Ted leaned back in his seat and exhaled all the bad air he'd been holding since takeoff. "See? I told you it would be better than walking."

She slapped him on the arm. "That was the shortest takeoff I've ever seen. You're supposed to protect me, not get me killed."

He thought she was serious, but when he glanced over, she smiled at him.

"What?" he asked.

Emily brushed hair out of her eyes. "That was incredible! I can't believe the Air Force made you sit in that back seat on Air Force Two. You're an amazing pilot."

He was going to reply, but he had to focus on flying. The river was broad and shallow, with rocks sticking out everywhere. Ahead, a long, thin island with four distinctive cooling towers hugged the left bank; a second island sat in the middle of the wide river. It would have been easy to fly above them, but he wanted the cover they provided, so he stayed low.

"Let's get by the Three Mile Island nuke plant," Ted suggested, "then we can celebrate."

San Francisco, CA

Dwight sat in the middle of the intersection for a long time. His brain often gave him conflicting information, so it was hard to say for sure, but he believed he was there for at least an hour. In that whole time, no one ran him over or kicked him as they walked across the street.

"See? That was a dumb idea, Poppy."

He listened to the bird talk.

"I don't know where they went. Let's go to the stadium to find out. That's where they come when they want hot dogs and popcorn." He listened again. "No, you can't have any!"

Dwight had trouble getting up. His legs had fallen asleep, though he'd barely noticed until he had to use them. Much of his body was like that. It had been more than a while since he'd been to a doctor.

Once he was on the move, it all came back to him. Walking became easier and less painful for his legs, and he almost enjoyed the stroll. Soon, he made it to the long street that would lead him to the stadium, which was visible a half-mile ahead.

As before, there wasn't a single car, person, or animal moving anywhere in this part of the city.

"What?" he replied to Poppy. "I'm not counting your kind." Birds continued to sit on power lines and in nearby trees. Pigeons walked ledges of buildings on each side, as they always did. It was beneath his notice, but not his pet bird's.

At some point in his long journey, he came across a friendly establishment.

"Victoria Hennessey's Wine and Beers."

Dwight looked both ways on the street. Still nothing.

"A short detour is in order." Poppy didn't complain, which was comforting. She used to bitch all the time about his fondness for the happy drinks, but that had gone away.

He walked unsteadily into the small shop, pleased to see no one inside. A person had tossed shirts and pants by the counter, but no one was standing there. An entire aisle of wine bottles was in the back.

"Maybe just one ..." He reached for whatever was first in the row. Poppy warned him against stealing, but he wasn't listening to her guidance in the face of such a bounty. It wasn't some random purse; it was the open bank vault.

His life became a blur of drinking "samples" he intended to pay for at a later date, as well as stuffing and organizing his survival gear for the remaining journey. He walked out loaded down with bottles inside two stout paper grocery bags.

He did make it to the stadium. He remembered that much. But there was no one there. It was 50,000 seats of empty. Poppy asked him to rest, so he took a seat on second base down on the baseball field.

When he finished another bottle, or spilled it—he wasn't sure—he ran the bases on the baseball diamond. He pulled out another bottle when he hit home plate.

From there, his blur became a near-blackout, though small snippets broke through the fog.

He spent time yelling at buildings after he'd left the stadium.

Another bottle was spent yelling at some yachts.

Finally, he came to his wits when his brain reminded him that he didn't know how to swim.

"I'm in the ocean, Poppy! Save me!"

His bird wasn't stupid enough to drown with him. She sat on a shipping container that had washed up on a rocky beach ahead of him. If he could figure out how to swim...

"Oh, wait." His foot touched something. "Ha! You tricked me." He struggled across the rock-strewn bottom and worked to get over to her. The city rose around him. The stadium was across a small inlet of the bay. He figured he'd left the stadium and walked right into the water.

A miracle got him the fifty yards to this side.

When he reached the shore, he realized there were victims of his mistake. The bags of wine were gone. Dwight looked into the water, hopeful they weren't far. All he had left was one bottle, which seemed to be glued in his grip. "At least you made it," he said to the bottle.

He felt the eyes of the bird watching him with disapproval, but he ignored them. "Poppy, fly around and find the other bottles!"

She remained on top of the beached shipping container.

He glared at her, but she wouldn't budge from her perch.

"Fine. I'll go back to the liquor store when I dry off." He walked onto shore but fell over right at the front door of the giant metal box. "But right now, I'm going to take a short nap."

The last thing he saw was Poppy flying down to land on him. Behind her, the shipping container doors were cracked open a little...

ELEVEN

Harrisburg, PA

"I've never seen a nuclear power plant from this angle," Emily remarked as the Cessna motored by the plant. They were above the water of the river, but still below the level of the huge concrete cooling towers.

"You didn't tour these things as part of your political junkets and whatever you did on the campaign trails?" He was being funny, because he no longer cared about her politics.

"These things are, pardon the pun, radioactive while out begging for votes. They scare people, even to this day. Politicians never want to be associated with things that scare voters, you know?"

"Just a little bit of fright, right? Like a balloon popping." He cracked up as the plant fell behind.

"Yeah. Only enough for them to reach out and ask for our help to keep the balloon from bursting. You've figured out the essence of my whole career."

He shook his head at the thought. "Well, we both need to figure out the next leg of our journey. No politics. No delays. We have to get you somewhere safe."

"What are our choices?" she asked.

Ted pointed in a circle around the plane. "We can go anywhere. We have a full tank of gas. If I remember right, that gives us about five hundred miles before we hit our reserve. Then, it's boom." He gestured a plane flying into the ground.

He wasn't as worried about range or running out of fuel. He could land the plane almost anywhere flat, including fields, highways, and beaches. All of those would be close while on the East Coast. His real fear was getting her captured. Their last close call reinforced his belief these troops were not friendly and weren't going to treat Emily kindly if they found her. Ted also didn't want to get himself captured, because he still needed to get to Kyla.

She made the first suggestion. "It's not five hundred miles to Canada. Maybe we could find help there?"

"Maybe," he allowed. "But when we were on board Air Force Two, we weren't picking up any signals up there, except way out on the Atlantic coast islands. I could be a hundred percent wrong, but I think that means their country suffered the same fate as the rest of North America."

Ted guided the plane down the center of the river channel, staying as low to the water as possible. He flew underneath giant powerlines, which probably came directly from the nuke plant. The guys back at the airport would almost certainly be looking for them, and it would be impossible to track them on radar if they were below the tree line. But that brought up another problem.

"We can't stay on this path. They'll know to look for us at the next town. The next highway crossing. Anything where they can see us along the river."

Emily seemed to mull it over. "So, our problem is getting somewhere where we know the people are friendly to us. DC is out. Harrisburg is out. Probably Baltimore and Richmond. Those are next in line from the capital. What about New York?"

"Do we know anyone in New York?" His sister had been there. "Who might be alive?" he added hastily.

"My husband was there," she replied without emotion. "We had an apartment in Manhattan and a house out on Long Island."

"I'm sorry," he said while guiding the plane over a particularly rocky section of the wide river. The boulders stuck up out of the water, suggesting a person could almost walk from one side to the other. He looked down, noting a few beach towels near shore. Evidence of the lost people followed him, even here.

"It's fine. I'm sure it will hit me when I least expect it, and I never wished harm to him, but we weren't close. It was more of a marriage of convenience, given how much our families were built around politics."

He held firm on the yolk but looked over with skepticism. "You don't seem like the type of gal who would put up with that."

There was barely an inch between them because the cabin was cramped. She shifted in her seat as if to get away from him. "And what kind of gal do I seem like?"

His brain screamed at him as surely as any alarm on the aircraft. Danger close.

"I didn't mean anything by it. Honest. It's just that the more I've gotten to know you, the less I see you as a politician and more as a person. I guess I've already forgotten a little about what the world was like before yesterday."

She gave him a sideways glance, but then got comfortable in her chair like she wanted to enjoy the ride.

He kept talking. "I think I can get us to New York, navigating by the terrain. I don't suppose you have a radio at your house on Long Island?"

Emily thought for a few seconds. "I wish we were in Montana. I bet my dad has all kinds of radios we could use."

"But nothing like that at your house?" It would be ideal if he could find a shortwave radio in a private residence. It would be less likely to attract attention than any base or government facility.

"Nope."

"All right. We'll stay with the river for a mile or two, then jump out and fly to the east. As long as we stay low, we should avoid detection from radar systems. I can follow the interstate, avoid Philadelphia, and eventually we'll see the New York skyline. From there, we can decide what we want to do. If we can find more fuel, maybe we can get up the coast and into Canada, like you said. We'll find the Canuck airport with the working tower we heard while on Air Force Two."

"And if we don't find fuel?"

He chuckled. "Let's not worry about that, yet. We've got five hundred miles until it becomes an issue."

The fuel gage showed they weren't quite at full anymore. He didn't remember this airframe being known for burning through fuel that fast, but he did abuse the throttle on takeoff. Maybe that was where it all went.

As he climbed above the trees at the edge of the river and turned east, he kept his eye on the fuel status as well as all the other instruments. However, he couldn't help but wonder if Emily had been truthful about not having feelings for her dead husband. If she didn't...

Danger close, for sure.

His mind bounced around with the turbulence outside. Getting to Kyla. Keeping the VP safe. Avoiding the assholes with guns. Anything but those improper thoughts.

Ted relaxed into his seat, appreciating the familiar pedals and yoke of the pilot's position.

Flying was the one thing in the day he could control.

St. Louis, MO

Tabby followed the sewer truck to an alleyway well out of view of the tractors and drones under the Arch. She pulled up behind them and turned off the car, immediately feeling helpless.

"We can't trust the people under the Arch, and we can't trust these two, either." She shifted in her seat in order to look to Peter and Audrey. "We can only trust each other, okay?"

"I trust you," Peter agreed, but then he tapped his shotgun. "I trust *Audrey Two* as well."

"Aww, you named your shotgun after me?" Audrey gushed.

Tabby's jaw fell open at the shock of seeing the exchange.

Peter beamed, proud of the gun in his arms.

The girl was being sarcastic, however. "There's something wrong with you, Pete."

He laughed, clearly unperturbed at her change of heart.

She wanted to get her message across before the men got out of their truck and came over.

"Keep *Audrey Two* on your shoulder, all right? We don't want to accidentally shoot these guys." She hesitated, then reiterated. "Say it with me: we don't want to accidentally shoot anyone."

Peter rolled his eyes. "Fine."

Audrey got out of the car, looking like she got the message as well.

Tabby opted not to carry her shotgun. It was big and awkward, and she didn't want to deal with it. However, she wasn't going out unarmed. She tucked the police-issue Glock into her pants behind her back, then made sure her shirt covered it.

The two sanitation workers stood behind their truck looking relaxed and unafraid. She gave them credit for that because she was nervous as hell around all the kids' guns, though she did her best to avoid showing that weakness.

"Looks like you four are taking this Apocalypse-thing seriously. Where'd you get all the firepower?" Gus pulled out a pack of smokes and put one in his mouth.

"A police station," Donovan replied. "She said we could keep them." He wore his police belt

153

over his sweatpants, similar to Peter and his get-up.

Tabby let out an uncertain chuckle. "I said they could keep them until we found the cordon."

Gus used a lighter on his cigarette, took in a long drag, then exhaled smoke. "Cordon? Where's that?"

"Is that where the people are?" his partner, Vinny, added. He was younger, maybe in his mid-twenties and wasn't quite as filthy as the older guy. He wore a clean St. Louis Blues hockey team hat, which was blue with a yellow musical note on the front. Underneath the rim, she briefly noted his big blue eyes.

Tabby kept on task. "It's where the police and fire departments have to be set up to receive people who are escaping this...disaster. I'm not sure if it was a fuel leak, poison gas, or what, but the four of us were in the Bonne Terre Mine when the gas tried to get us."

Gus lit up. "We were down below, too. Working on a seal job deep under the Met Square building. Goofball, here, let one of the doors close behind us, so we couldn't get out for half the day yesterday."

Tabby watched Vinny for his reaction; he seemed upset at himself.

She continued, assuming she knew how the story ended. "And when you came up top, everyone was gone?"

He nodded. "We drove back to the metro sewer shed and found nothing but abandoned vehicles there."

"And clothes," Vinny added.

Gus nodded with the interplay between his partner. "Yeah, and clothes. It was like everyone decided to have a little fun before they abandoned this world."

"They got away," she corrected.

"Sure, kid. They got away." Gus puffed out more smoke. "So, after we had our fill of being abandoned down here on the streets, we went up to the top of the nearest hotel to watch the whole city. We spent as much time as we could watching the river for boats, the air for planes, and the ground for any living thing."

"Boats? Did you see any?"

He looked disappointed. "We saw a few. Barges came shooting down the river like they always did, but these were evidently driverless. They struck the bridges as they came through, cracking up collections of cargo barges. It set them free and they floated downstream, hitting every bridge and dock they passed."

Vinny silently nodded.

"And you didn't see anyone since yesterday?"

"We didn't see anyone..." Gus trailed off, then took a heavy drag on his cigarette.

The younger guy glanced over. "We can tell them."

Gus seemed to steel himself before continuing. "Until this morning...when they showed up." He pointed toward the Arch grounds, though they couldn't see it from the alley. "At first, it was a lone tractor down there. Then a couple of those flying drones swooped in. Vinny and I were amped up to go down there and be glad we found someone, but another MSD truck beat us to it."

"There are more of you?" Peter asked with surprise. "What are the odds?" He didn't sound like he believed the story.

Gus took offense to his tone. "We work in some fecal-positive conditions, kid. You'd be surprised how messy it can get with all your generation using baby wipes on your coddled bottoms. Those things clog up the tunnels like giant corks. We can spend days picking those apart."

Vinny visibly shuddered.

"Anyway, another crew must have been working underground when people disappeared. We watched as they sped across the grass to the guys under the Arch, almost like you did. A pair of MSD workers got down from their truck, then went over to the new people. The men in the tractors hopped out too, but when they met up, they shot our friends."

"Were they threatening them?" Peter suggested.

Gus held up his hands to show they were empty. "We work in the sewers, kid. Other than smelling like we've been stomping toilet wine down below, do we look like threats to you?"

Peter said something in response, but Tabby noticed movement at the end of the alley that made her body lock up like she'd been caught in freeze tag. She tried to speak, but her mouth wouldn't open.

Gus continued, oblivious to her issue. "They put the two workers back in their truck, then drove it down the cobblestones and right into the Mississippi..."

A white drone hovered along the connecting street about fifty feet away. It went from her right to her left, and though she expected it to turn and look at her every second it was there, it glided silently out of sight.

She pointed at the empty street and eked out a whisper.

"Guys, a drone just went by."

TWELVE

Poor Sisters Convent, Oakville, MO

Rose left Biscuit the black lab in her house. As soon as she closed the door, the excitable pup ran to the front window and began barking again. This time, she saw her wagging tail, so she didn't seem threatening. She only wanted someone to play with.

The entire street had dogs anxious to get out and play. And eat.

"We have to go back," she advised Deogee.

The gray wolf-dog was reluctant to leave her new friend, but once Rose left the lab's front yard, she followed without a leash.

"You really are a good dog," she said to her companion.

On the way home, Rose let her friend visit the yellow sneakers of her old master again, but the pup didn't spend as much time there. Soon enough, she followed her across the yard and up the front walkway.

Rose searched for the source of the earlier noise in the air, but it was nowhere to be seen. She figured she'd missed her chance to see it by being up the street rather than at home. Still, she couldn't sit inside and wait. She resolved to go to the pet store, if only to buy food for Deogee and the lonely lab, though she knew it wouldn't end there.

"I'll only be a minute," she said to encourage the dog not to be afraid.

Rose went in and found the key chain in Abbess Mary Francis' belongings. She said a short prayer for her former leader, then walked back out the front door.

Deogee ran laps around the trees in the yard, like she was still playing with the lab. It was an impressive display too, because she was very fast. But Rose also remembered the press of the clock; those dogs hadn't eaten since yesterday morning.

"Come on, Deogee! Come!"

The wolf ripped around the trunk of the tree and came right at her. She bared her teeth and looked ferocious, making Rose wonder about her intentions, but she slowed down and almost skidded to a stop in the grass. Her tail wagged uncontrollably, like her human pal was about to hand out treats.

"Good dog! Now, get in here." She opened the sliding side door of the abbess's minivan.

She jumped up and got on the backseat without complaint. The old Sister Rose would have been mortified at how it could scratch the vinyl seats, but she took it in stride. She ensured the dog was inside, then shut the door.

Rose walked around to the front and opened her door to get in. Deogee waited for her from the passenger seat in the front.

"You want to ride next to me, huh?" She didn't think it mattered. "Fine."

As she got in and buckled herself, she lowered the windows to give the dog some air. Deogee pawed at her and licked her face while she worked the controls with her left hand.

"You're welcome!" she laughed. After enduring as many kisses as she could stand, Rose pushed the pup onto the other seat. "This is for safety, okay?"

When she turned around to face the steering wheel, she was scared out of her wits by a mechanical object hovering outside the open driver's window.

"Oh heavens!"

The futuristic-looking contraption hovered with the assistance of four small fans. It looked like a child's skateboard with circular blades on each corner. It also had a tennis-ball-sized black orb hung underneath, and a tiny speaker.

"Please identify yourself," a computer voice requested.

Pennsylvania Countryside

Ted and Emily had been flying for about an hour before she noticed their fuel situation.

"When were you going to tell me?" she said matter-of-factly.

"I wasn't sure until about five minutes ago," he replied. Their fuel was already below half a tank, which shouldn't have happened for another hour. That bullet had, in fact, penetrated the plane, even though they couldn't see the hole from where they were. And, because Murphy's Law enjoyed flying, the bullet had gone into one of the two fuel tanks inside the wings. "I've been thinking how I can tell you without worrying you."

Her laughter was tense. "I've been worried since yesterday. I doubt I could be any more concerned for our safety. I can handle it."

"Oh, I'm sure of that. You're a tough cookie. However, I'm protecting the President of the United States. I don't want to foul this up."

She reached over and put her hand on his. "You won't. I won't let you. Now, you've just told me, so what do we do now?"

He'd never stopped worrying, either, but sharing it bled off a tiny fraction of the stress he'd been saving up in his clenched jaw. "We're going to have to put down and find another aircraft. Every little airport across America will have these Cessna 172s and other small craft."

She pulled her hand back and looked out the window. "I wish we could take a big plane. That would get us there faster. Maybe even across the ocean. But we can't..."

"No, we might be able to get a slightly bigger plane in the air, but then it would be harder to fly and easier to spot on radar. If we went out into the Atlantic, we'd have to deal with those missile boats, too. I say we keep going up the coast, like we'd planned."

"So, what are we going to do about this doomed flight?"

"Do you see an airport?" he joked. "We should probably do this sooner rather than later. New York City is on the horizon. Once we get there, we'll only have big airports to deal with. Might be harder to find little civilian planes."

"So, where do we go?" she wondered aloud.

"I think we'll be fine at Newark. It's a little short of New York. It will make a nice turning point before we go north again. And the best part is, we should be heading right for it."

He kept talking as the plane soared at about fifty feet above the fields and trees below.

"Before we land, I want you to cover your face. We don't know if they're already on the ground in New Jersey, or not. We might have to land and run. If that happens, it would be better for both of us if the bad guys didn't know who you were."

"They won't chase us if they think I'm Julie Six-Pack?"

He shrugged. "I guarantee if they knew who was on this plane, they'd be covering every airport within our service range."

"I'll do like this." She pulled her arm up to her face, essentially hiding herself like Dracula.

Ted rolled his eyes. "You know, for a vice president, you sure don't take much seriously, you know that?"

She laughed. "I told you, humor is what keeps me sane. It keeps me from thinking about what could be out there looking for us. It helps me forget all those cars and houses down there are now empty." She looked at him from behind her mask. "It helps me endure not being told we're running out of fuel."

"Yeah, about that—"

"See, I told you," she interjected. "Humor is what's going to help me survive being with you."

"Am I really that bad?"

Her eyes conveyed the smile hidden behind her elbow and she talked in a Dracula voice. "Find me another plane and all will be right again."

As New York filled the landscape, the comparatively small airport at Newark appeared as a large flat area not far ahead. A great fire burned several miles to the north of the field, inside what looked like a sea of houses. It was probably fueled by the millions of garages, cans of lawnmower gasoline, and flammable home decor inside each structure.

He was about to tell her he had his target, in the spirit of openness, but he caught sight of movement on the airfield, causing him to change his message.

"We have to land right now!"

Ted jammed the nose down and searched for an alternative landing strip.

The airport ahead was already full.

Amarillo, TX

Brent led the charge of four vehicles across the flat grassland north of Amarillo. He was in the lead, his big F-250 belching diesel fumes as he jammed the pedal to the floor on the empty two-lane blacktop.

Paul and Cliff were in the green sedan behind him. Ross and Kevin were in a second pickup truck. Carter was in his friend Greer's old Volkswagen bug.

And the prisoners were armed to the teeth. Once he opened the armory, he had to accept they would take everything they could. Each man readily accepted a riot shotgun and a Glock 22. They didn't shoot him in the back when he walked out, nor did they harm him while he found keys for the cars on the lot, so he figured he was in the clear.

"I'm lucky they're coming with me," he said to himself. He wanted them in separate vehicles to give the appearance there were more than seven of them. He wanted to storm Trish's place and scare the attackers away, if he could.

His rig downshifted as he turned into Trish's dusty gravel street. Her trailer park wasn't much more than one short road with ten single-wides clinging to the earth inside a protective clump of trees, surrounded by endless grasslands.

Trish's trailer was obvious because of the three or four trucks parked around it.

"Dammit all," he drawled. "I should have known some of them would be interested in the one beautiful young woman they knew was still alive." His ploy to use numbers wasn't going to work.

He touched a small cross hanging from his rearview mirror. He prayed God would be his co-pilot outside the truck, too.

The other vehicles pulled up behind his, but he was out and running up the front steps before his pals had gathered behind him. There might not be an extra second to waste.

"Trish!" he shouted.

He racked the shotgun as he got onto the top step.

"Open up!"

When the door opened, it wasn't any prisoner he expected to see.

"Curtis?"

"What do you want, boss man? You let us go." Curtis watched as Brent's backup arrived, but he didn't seem worried.

Curtis wasn't someone he ever thought of as trouble. He was young and stupid, like most of the guys, but he seemed willing to work hard in the prison so he could get out in a few months and get back to his real life. Now he wore a teal bandana and had a pistol wedged into the front of his pants. One hand sat on the bottom of the grip.

"Trish said there were uninvited guests giving her trouble here. Is she okay?" He tried to look past the guy, but the inside of the place was dark. The curtains were drawn, and the lights were off.

Curtis frowned. "Did you boys come with this law-dog? If so, me and my gang might have something to say about it."

Brent half-turned to greet them, expecting them to back him up.

"Hell no," Paul said. "We've been chasing him since the prison. He ran out the door to rescue his babe, but he left the armory doors open. We've got all the guns!"

Paul held up his shotgun to show it off.

"Traitor," Brent said under his breath.

That made Curtis laugh. "What's the matter, boss? You re-thinking letting us all go?"

He tried to keep his cool. "You were a good kid, son. You almost cleared your six months. You would have been back out in no time, getting life back together."

They'd spoken often about how the young man wanted to get his GED certificate to finish high school more than anything. He even mentioned wanting to go into the corrections industry to help other inmates.

"Dude. You don't get it. Life out here is brutal. I'm in a gang, not your fairy tale world where I get a degree and do something lame." He motioned back in the house. "We're all in a gang now. Mine."

"Dammit, you have the whole of Amarillo to take from. Why are you here with Officer Perez?"

Brent didn't dwell on the fact his crew had hardcore betrayed him. He would die trying to protect his friend. Curtis had surprised him, but he could end his life with a quick flick of his shotgun barrel.

"She's nice," Curtis agreed. "Come inside and I'll show you what we've got lined up for her."

The kid he once thought of as bright now seemed dark and sinister. Someone who deserved to take a blast of buckshot in the teeth.

He was about to do it, too, when he felt the barrel of a gun in the small of his back. Another man grabbed his shotgun and made him lower it.

Paul brushed his wavy hair aside and motioned for him to give up his guns. "Let's go inside, boss. See what Curtis has in store for you and your lovely friend. I believe I'm interested in the last woman left alive, too."

Curtis laughed. "Bring him in, guys."

171

THIRTEEN

Newark, NJ

"The Newark airport is already being taken over," he said dryly, searching out his window for somewhere to land. "If they're in the tower, we might have showed up on radar as we got close." It was hard to stay at treetop level as they entered the suburban sprawl. Sometimes they had to go over treeless hills or avoid tangles of high-tension power lines.

She braced herself as Ted descended as far as he dared. "They think we're going to land there?"

He craned his neck, looking out every window. "Yep. Probably figured they'd grab us when we got there. We have to get on the ground before they realize we've had a change of heart. Let me know if you see anything."

They both watched the ground. They'd already been flying low, but now they were only high enough to avoid chimney tops.

The good news was that they were now on the western edge of the metropolis of New York City and there was a little of everything below. He could pick a landing site from among the long stretches of interstate, the golf courses, or the many huge parking lots.

"I'd go for the highway," she remarked.

He'd been thinking along those lines. A golf course would be perfect if they wanted to get out of sight immediately, but fairways could have overhanging trees or sand traps. Either could be deadly.

The highway would make it impossible to hide the plane, but the level pavement would be a safer place to put down.

"There's where we're headed." He pointed to a long stretch of interstate twelve lanes wide. The plane banked left as he lined up his approach.

"Watch the street signs," she advised.

As he got aligned with the roadway, he tried to see out her window toward the airport. No planes were in the air, but some giant transports were taxiing on the ground. Nothing that big would risk landing without tower support; someone had to be watching he and Emily.

"We've got to get out as fast as possible, okay? Grab as much gear as you can, then run like hell for the houses." They were coming down in the middle of an ocean of single-family homes. The highway cut through suburbia like a narrow bridge on its way to the island of Manhattan. Its tall skyscrapers stood in for tropical palm trees fifteen hazy miles away.

Ted adjusted the choke and flaps as he guided the Cessna over the highway. There were a lot of cars on the eastbound lanes, but almost none going westbound. He'd seen the rush hour traffic pattern back in DC, too.

"Hang on," he said in his pilot's voice.

The nimble little plane went down below the trees lining the highway, and he was about to commit when he realized a wrecked car might be a little too close on the right side. He drifted at about ten feet until he got by, then he let the plane bleed off the last of its altitude.

The three tires of the landing gear hit concrete a few seconds later, and he engaged the brakes after just a moment.

"Touchdown!" he exhaled. Every landing had the potential to be his last, so Ted treated each one with a great deal of respect. "Air Force One is on the ground."

She chuckled with her own sense of relief. "We really doing this? Calling me the president?"

Ted goosed the motor to carry them down the highway toward the next overpass. If he could put the plane under there, he might be able to avoid detection from the air. It wasn't something he'd considered while in the air, but it was obvious once he was down.

"Until I hear differently, I'm going to treat you as the most important person in America. You are the only woman I know for an absolute fact is still alive and is in line to be president."

She seemed to consider it for a few moments. When Ted got the plane into the shade of the wide overpass, she sighed with relief. "This was smart thinking, pilot. Can you see about getting me a de-boarding staircase so I can climb down? The president deserves that, don't you think?"

He guided the plane into the shoulder of the highway and pointed it at the sloped embankment under the bridge, so it was out of the way of most of the lanes. If cars did go by, they wouldn't bash into the Cessna. He figured the owner would appreciate that.

Ted opened the door, then jumped out. As he grabbed his gear from behind the seat, he watched Emily do the same. He wanted to joke around with her, but this was the most dangerous time for them both.

He'd pulled out his backpack, but before he could sling his AR over his shoulder and get moving, the engine whine of another aircraft came in on the breeze. It was a single-prop plane like the Cessna, but the drone wasn't the same.

"Aw, shit," he drawled.

Emily looked at him from across the front seats. "Let me guess..."

He shrugged. "They have to be on to us." They hadn't seen any other aircraft during the flight, but now there was one snooping around.

When all the other people of America were gone, meeting someone wasn't a coincidence.

The propeller rumble got closer and suddenly he was at a loss for the sure thing to do. They were under the overpass, but they were visible from the sides. Their large, white plane was impossible to miss for anyone looking for it.

He got her attention. "Get your stuff. We've got to move."

She scrambled to pull out her rifle and ammo pouch. He slung his AR and put himself behind the door as the plane cruised over the highway about a quarter of a mile away.

"It's a Piper Cherokee. Six-seater, I think."

Emily seemed to have trouble getting her rifle from the backseat, but he didn't move until the plane went out of sight. Once it was gone, he stepped away from the door and ran around the tail to get over to her.

"Go, Emily. We've got to get away from this plane."

She yanked her rifle out. "The sling got stuck on the seat."

He gently shoved her away from the door.

Emily hustled, but she also turned back like she'd forgotten something. "Hey! Where's my staircase? This airport is getting a strongly-worded letter."

Ted appreciated what she was trying to do.

The lawnmower-engine whine of the search plane came at them from one direction, but there was also another motor higher up. His pilot's eye picked it out of the sky: a long, swept-wing Predator drone.

"Shi—" he started to cuss, before realizing he didn't want to frighten her unnecessarily. "Come on, we—" He saw the puff of smoke. A missile fell off the wing and flew in a graceful arc right at them.

Scaring her was unavoidable.

"Run!"

St. Louis, MO

Tabby and the kids ran behind her gold-colored Ford to hide from the drone. The two men moved with less haste, but they also crouched behind her car. Tabby's focus was on waiting for the drone to come back, but she glanced at the men to make sure they were down. Gus's attention appeared mostly on his cigarette, but his eyes also went to Audrey's shotgun.

She immediately gave up waiting for the drone; her duty was to the children. "We have to get in touch with someone on the outside. Does your truck have a radio?" She peered at Gus.

The dirt-covered sewer worker took a stiff drag on his cigarette, then shifted smoothly from Audrey to her. The smoke came out of his lungs as he spoke. "We could only talk to dispatch, but we haven't been able to raise them. Before you ask, we've tried calling the police from the hotel, too."

Audrey coughed from the second-hand smoke.

Tabby had to do something. The two men seemed harmless enough, but that wouldn't last long. She expected Gus to ask for a weapon any second, and it would be hard to justify not giving him one, because she and the kids had extras. If she had to tell them no, it would make things even more uncomfortable than they already were.

Vinny inched closer to her. "We did a job below the Channel 5 television building not too long ago. It's a few blocks away. They might have communications equipment." He smiled at Tabby. Unlike Gus, she got a good feeling from him.

"Yeah, we should do that. Let's go that way." She pointed away from the end of the alley where she'd seen the floating drone.

Peter leaned close to her. "Are we sure these guys are telling the truth? Maybe the people flying the drones are here to help us. Unlike them."

Gus laughed. "We can hear you, kid."

Peter didn't back down. "We have the guns. I'm not afraid of you."

"Your pointer should be on the side of the guard, not on the trigger, boy." Gus's eyes made a dotted line to Peter's finger, which was on the trigger. She'd have to remember that advice, even if it came from a sketchy man.

"It's okay." Tabby put her hand on Peter's shotgun. He wasn't pointing it at anyone, but he did have both hands on it, like it was open for business. "Who would lie about people dying from their company? Besides, the guys under the Arch didn't exactly have a Red Cross tent to welcome us in."

"Fine," Peter pouted. "Let's find the TV station and get this over with."

Tabby's heart rattled inside her ribcage because everyone was acting unpredictably. If she was going to keep her kids safe, she had to keep the tour moving. She forced a smile toward Gus and Vinny. "I'm sorry for this. Yesterday, we learned their parents weren't able to get out. I hope you understand. It isn't you."

Gus took another drag. "Bah. I get it. We'll drive behind you guys."

"No!" she blurted. "We can't drive." The little drone might have been gone, but they'd gotten lucky it hadn't looked down the narrow alley. Being on foot would better allow them to hide if they saw it again, she was fairly certain.

Gus harrumphed. "What the hell do you want from us?"

Vinny nudged Gus. "The station is only a few blocks from here—a ten-minute walk, at best. When we get there, we can report those bastards for killing our co-workers."

The older man seemed to think on it as he burned through his cigarette. Tabby was on the verge of leaving them both behind, but he finally nodded. "We'll keep the truck where it is. I'll call in to dispatch and let them know our intentions, just in case we don't get back in a timely fashion. I'll meet you at the other end of the alley."

Tabby stood up and marshalled the kids together. "Works for us."

She practically pushed Donovan ahead of her. "What's the rush?" he asked.

"Just walk," she insisted.

About halfway down the alley, she gathered them together. "Watch that Gus. He's up to something. I didn't like the way he looked at Audrey's gun."

Peter hugged his shotgun. "Nobody's getting my *Audrey Two*."

She smiled. "You watch him, okay, Peter? I'm putting you in charge of that."

Tabby had more to say, but Vinny trotted up. He immediately spoke to her in a quiet way. "I'm sorry about him. I think that shooting messed him up. We really were about to go down there ourselves. He's been with MSD forever, so he probably knew whoever was killed, though he refuses to talk about it."

She did her best not to betray her own feelings of mistrust. Vinny didn't need to know; he might tell his friend. "We're anxious, too. If we can get in contact with someone, I'm sure we can straighten this all out." She spoke a bit quieter, almost to herself. "I want this to all be over."

"It's going to be all right," the young man said sympathetically. "I can tell you guys are going to make it through this. You seem like a tough girl."

She blushed with embarrassment, but her demeanor shifted as Gus arrived. No matter what she thought of Vinny, and his distracting blue eyes, she couldn't allow anything to take her concentration off job number one.

"Kids, stick with me. Vinny is going to lead us."

He walked ahead. "We keep going that way."

They reached the end of the alley between the two buildings. Ahead, a wide avenue stood between them and another alleyway on the far side.

Vinny took off his hat and peeked around the corner but yanked his head back an instant later. "We've got company headed this way."

Her stomach hit the panic button.

She suddenly wished she'd brought the shotgun.

FOURTEEN

Newark, NJ

A long time ago, Kyla and Mom took a ride in one of Uncle Ted's little planes, but she had never been in a helicopter, so the flight on the big military machine was another notch in her training. After being up in the air for only a short time, she appreciated again why her uncle flew for a living; the view was incredible.

They'd been flying above the ocean for about twenty minutes before they turned inland. As soon as they did, Meechum reached over and tapped her, then spoke through the industrial-grade headset and mic gear they both wore. "Can you hear me?" Meechum asked at nearly a scream.

Kyla scrambled to turn down the volume. She gave the Marine a thumbs-up once she did.

"This is where I need you. We're starting to go over Staten Island, New Jersey. We're going to sweep to the north and east to see if we can find any survivors."

"So... I just look outside?"

Meechum grinned. "Not everything about being a warrior is fun."

"I don't mind," she said dryly. The less drama, the better.

They flew above thousands of houses, and there were many more to the west. It was like one big subdivision that went from the edge of the coast all the way to the curve of the horizon. The rivers and bays and skyscrapers of Manhattan were to the north. She'd recognize that skyline anywhere; that's where Mom lived.

Used to live. Does live. Maybe lives?

She'd accepted something big had happened to the world, including people and sailors who disappeared into thin air, but she wasn't ready to accept it had taken her mother. If she could just see the city was all right...

Kyla lost some of her enthusiasm for a brief time, but she couldn't let it drag her too far down. As Meechum stated, it wasn't all fun and games. She'd been brought up here to do a job.

The helicopter was low enough for her to see trash cans at the end of driveways, individual windows on cars, and colorful lawn chairs sitting poolside in many of the backyards. She imagined if there were people down there, they'd be easy to spot, but, at first glance, no one came running out to greet them.

"If you see anything interesting, let me know and I'll let the pilot know. You know?" Meechum laughed.

Kyla let herself lean toward the open doorway but kept one hand on the seat belt. It would put her closer to danger, but it made it possible to see almost directly below them. If people were down there, she didn't want to miss them.

Meechum sat on the floor of the cargo hold, with her legs dangling outside the aircraft. As usual, she made it look easy.

"You can do that, too," she told herself.

They flew for a couple of minutes before she gathered up the fortitude necessary to try it. She found the tether rope attached to the wall, then buckled herself in with a carabiner.

She breathed fast, like she was about to dive underwater.

"You can do this," she whispered.

Kyla unhitched her seatbelt and set it aside. She slid off the edge of the seat, never losing contact with it as she got onto the floor.

"Just a little more," she encouraged herself.

The heavy rope would prevent her from falling out the door. She knew that. However, it seemed like the most dangerous thing she'd ever thought of doing. The earth flew by below her. One fall and she'd be dead.

Still, she got her feet over the edge and carefully shimmied her legs over the side, too. Gradually, she slid even closer until everything below her knees was out of the helicopter.

"I did it!" she said to herself. Uncle Ted wouldn't believe she'd flown today, much less stuck her feet out the door of a moving helicopter.

"I could get used to flying," she said in her microphone.

Meechum agreed. "It's amazing, isn't it? Do you see anything over there? I don't see nothin' on this side."

Her attention had been elsewhere while she'd gotten down onto the floor, but now she made a concerted effort to do her job. At first, there was nothing to look at but more houses, streets, and tree-covered yards. Far to the north, a huge fire consumed a large part of the landscape. The black smoke rose to the stratosphere like a towering thunderhead.

"That thing is out of control," she said.

Somehow, the Marine knew what she meant. "If you ever wondered if you should pay your fire department, this should be your clue."

The fire was the most interesting thing out there, but her vision was drawn to movement in the air a lot closer. An orange spark and a puff of smoke appeared between her and the rager.

"I see something!" she yelled.

The orange streak went downward and closed distance on a highway. Before she had time to comment on it, the missile exploded under a bridge, and flames and black smoke burst from both sides of the overpass.

A man's voice interrupted her thoughts. "Evade!" the pilot yelled three times in a row.

The airframe dipped as the pilot steered them away from whatever shot that missile. She had half a second to wonder what had been struck down there, but her whole life flashed in front of her eyes as she slid right out the door.

Newark, NJ

The Hellfire missile crashed into the Cessna about ten seconds after they'd run away from it. The concussion knocked them both to the ground, but Ted scrambled to his feet as fast as he was able.

"Come on, hurry!" He pointed at the enemy's Piper Cherokee. It was lining up a landing on the interstate, exactly as he and Emily had done.

Emily's eyes lolled for a moment, but she focused on him. "Did I fall?"

"Yeah," he laughed. "You were clumsy. Let's get up and run."

He had to help her up, but once she'd gotten upright, her balance improved.

"What happened?" she asked, like she'd regained her senses.

"Drone attack. These guys aren't messing around. We've got to get out of here before more bad guys show up."

The whirr of the Piper steadily rose as it came closer. He watched as it descended toward the highway. He and Emily stood on top of the embankment, giving them some concealment, but he wanted to get her running toward the nearby suburban homes, so he tugged at her elbow.

That got her moving.

They made it to the back yard of the first house on the street as tires chirped on the highway. The plane was below their line of sight, because the interstate sat in a lowered channel, but there was no mistaking how close the aircraft was.

Ted ran through the yard and came out on a short block of homes with a white-steepled church at the end. The small brick homes appeared clean and tasteful with stubby driveways and narrow porches. It was the type of place where he might have lived if he wasn't an apartment person, always on the move.

He looked both ways on the street, frantic to find evidence of a car that had lost its driver.

"We want a ride, right?" she asked, apparently catching on.

He ran toward the intersection at the end of the street. "We have to get out of here fast. They're coming."

If he'd planned to make a stand, his best bet would have been to shoot into the plane as it landed. However, the Predator drone usually traveled with two Hellfire missiles. There could also be a hundred drones behind that one. His priority was escaping that to get Emily out of danger, not to inflict casualties on the enemy.

They made it to the end of the street. To the right, the road went underneath the highway. To the left, it went into the suburban neighborhood.

There were several cars on the side of the road, or in the yards of nearby homes.

"That one!" he pointed to a boxy sedan parked against a hedge nearby. After a short run, he hopped inside, but it wouldn't start. "Out of gas. It must have run dry idling since yesterday. We need a stick shift."

"Why?" she pressed.

"When drivers, uh, went away, they couldn't work the clutches. The motors would die when the RPMs got too low. That's our advantage right now." He saw a sporty car about a hundred yards away. "Go for that one!"

They hopped back out and ran along the sidewalk. He only checked back once to make sure she was on his tail. He had the heavy backpack, so he was sure she could keep up with him.

The hum of the Predator came from all around them, as if the sound waves bounced off the roofs and walls of the houses. There was also the whir of a helicopter in the distance. He was sure of it.

"They've got all kinds of gear after us," he remarked.

Emily breathed heavily as she ran alongside him. "Are we going to hide?"

It was tempting to go into one of the houses close by. Several had their garages open, and probably their doors; people had been hanging around outside when the event took their lives, but he didn't diverge from his goal.

"Not yet. We can't stay around here. They'd eventually find us."

She stumbled with an "oops" but quickly regained her footing. The sidewalk was a little older on this wider street, and some of the cracks had grown quite large.

"You okay?" he asked with a quick glance over his shoulder.

"Right behind you."

They made it to the black sports car. It had run up on a curb, but otherwise seemed unharmed. He yanked out a woman's slacks and a shirt. The former owner wouldn't need them anymore.

Emily slid into the leather passenger seat a moment later.

"This feels familiar. We keep getting chased."

He noticed she didn't have anything over her face, so he cracked open his door and picked up the woman's blouse. "Take this. Use it to make a mask. We have to hide your identity for as long as possible, and I don't think you can do your Dracula thing while holding a rifle."

"What about you?" she asked with concern.

He depressed the clutch and started the engine, since the keys were already in the ignition.

"Please make one for me, too."

As he said it, the Predator drone appeared from the same direction he'd seen it before. It cruised low and slow, like it was searching for something to shoot. He knew an operator was sitting in a faraway room looking at live video feed of the neighborhood around them. He and Emily might already be designated as a target.

"Get down!" he ordered.

San Francisco, CA

Dwight was drunk as a skunk, but he'd found his new home.

"I declare this Dwight's Hideaway!" he cried out.

The blue shipping container had some foreign characters on the outside, and it was slanted a little because the back part was at the lower part of the beach, but he figured it was almost the perfect place to live. It had four cots bolted to both walls toward the front. There was a small cupboard in the middle of one wall, and that was filled with canned foods. A toolbox was latched onto the floor next to it. About fifteen seats stuck out of the floor toward the back, making three neat rows. At the very rear, a curtain blocked off a five-gallon bucket used for sanitation. He could live in there for a month.

For a short time, he lounged on a low cot, but eventually, he had to try the four on his wall. Then he tried all of them on the other side, certain one had to be better than the others.

"They're not all the same," he said to Poppy.

The bird laughed at him, causing him to give up his research. Instead, he sat in one of the plastic seats and started on his last wine bottle.

Once he'd made good headway, Poppy stared at him as she liked to do.

"Not this again. You saw it out there; the whole city has left us."

He remembered thinking about what might have caused it, but his liquor-addled brain couldn't remember the details. However, Poppy wanted to know.

Dwight leaned his head over the back of the chair and stared at the lone bulb tied to the ceiling. "I once met a guy who worked for the Air Force. Said he was part of a secret department that worked in New Mexico somewhere. I—"

He turned to Poppy. "No, I don't remember where. It's not important.

"Anyway, he always said aliens were real and the rest of us would know they were real when they finally chose to make an appearance. He said it would be big and impossible to miss. I'm calling it: the whole city got into an alien spaceship."

Poppy was silent, which he took as an insult.

"You think you know better?"

He hopped out of his chair. "We need to secure this home against invasion! Aliens. Dinosaurs. I don't care what. Nothing can get through that door if we lock it." It had a latch to hold it shut, but he wanted a better way to block it.

Dwight scoured the inside of the container for something he could use to bolt the door, but there wasn't much in the way of resources. The toolbox had a small hammer, some screwdrivers, and a can of orange spray paint. Nothing to brace both doors together.

"Oh, it doesn't matter," he said with defeat. "If the world has been invaded by aliens, I'm sure they can get inside one last shipping box, don't you?

"What?" He studied the blank spot on his shoulder, where the bird sat. "You think that would work?"

He picked up the can of spray paint and shook it. The rattle-can ball echoed inside the confinement of the shipping container. After a suitable amount of time, he pushed through the doors to the outside.

It took him several minutes to get all the words on the side of the container visible from the beach, but when he was done, he was proud of his efforts. Dwight ran up the sandy bank toward a nearby road. He laughed out loud when he saw the results of his efforts. "Poppy, you're a genius."

He'd painted *Free Candy Inside.*

He snickered, knowing it would scare every normal person away. It was impossible to know what the aliens would think, but it was a start.

"All right, Poppy, you got me outside to do this one thing. Now I'm going back inside to sleep off this nightmare."

He walked with determination back to his home, but he was a little more sober than he was the previous time he'd gone in. Now, it was evident there had been people inside the box before him. A long line of heavy boot prints started outside the container and went up the beach.

Dwight stood there for so long, he lost any sense of time. It was as if his brain turned off, then came back when it wanted to.

"No!" he yelled to Poppy. "I'm not going to follow those tracks."

FIFTEEN

Newark, NJ

"Don't move," Ted advised as the drone crossed over the street about a half-mile away. He turned off the motor, hoping the heat signature of running it for a few seconds wouldn't give them away. "They can't look everywhere, but they're almost for sure going to be looking at roads closest to what's left of our plane."

Emily tucked herself into the floorboard but leaned over the center console toward him. "Are you sure we should get in a car if they're looking for us this hard already?"

The Predator drone soon went out of his line of sight, though the engine purr indicated it wasn't gone for good. He'd never piloted one of those drones, but he assumed they'd fly in a regular pattern and search the streets with some semblance of order. Once he and Emily got into the car, they'd be committed to getting out of the hot zone. To do that, he'd need to go somewhere they could get lost.

"Those men landing in the plane are going to track us on foot. The guys above are going to be there when we're found. Something is happening around here, and we've got to get clear of it before they search every house."

He pointed east. "Our best bet is to get lost in New York City."

She breathed hard from their run, but still managed to chuckle. "Sounds like a love song."

Ted let himself smile. "The drone won't be able to spot us as easily, and they'd need an army to check every building where they thought we were. Besides, as long as they don't know who you are, I think they'll simply let us go if we make it that far."

Emily blew some fallen bangs out of her eyes, making him briefly acknowledge her as a pretty lady, rather than his boss. She looked right at him. "No offense, but that doesn't sound likely."

He shrugged, getting back to business. "It's the best I've got. We can't fight a whole army with two rifles and some matches. We need to get around them. This is the best way to do it."

Ted listened for the drone engine to grow quiet, but it hung around over the suburban neighborhood close by. He slowly started the engine again, as if the act of turning it on would alert the world.

"I think the nearby highway goes into the city. One of the signs we missed during the landing said it was thirty miles away."

She got back into her seat. "That sounds far."

Ted put the car into gear and enjoyed the rumble of the powerful motor. Much as he did with the stolen plane, he looked over the controls on the dashboard.

"We've got more than enough fuel. All we have to do is avoid detection and we should be in the city within thirty minutes."

She scoffed. "Have you never been to New York? Thirty miles could take you all day back when traffic was cooking."

"I have, lots of times. I guess I'm an optimist. But yeah, well, let's see." He stepped on the gas and the raw power of the Camaro shot up his leg as the car rolled off the curb and into the street. The black color would hide them a bit and he immediately went to the far side of the road, in the wrong lane, to better keep the houses between him and wherever the drone flew in that direction. At the first cross street, he sped through the intersection, but he slowed at the next one because it had the shield-shaped sign for the interstate.

"Almost there," he whispered.

Ted slowed as he took the turn but punched it on the next stretch of open surface road. The throaty roar of the big-block Chevy gave him a false sense of confidence he found hard to squelch. *You can never have too much horsepower*, his dad used to say back in his muscle-car years during the 1980s. Ted believed he could outrun anything.

The interstate on-ramp beckoned him toward danger, but he passed the on-ramp, went under the highway, and turned onto what was normally the exit ramp for westbound traffic. Two giant red 'Wrong Way' signs faced him as he started up the hill.

"Here we go," he said dryly.

"Should I have my rifle ready?" she asked. "I'll shoot down a plane if I have to."

He shifted through the gears and eased them up to seventy-five without much effort, and he was close to ninety when he got up the ramp and onto the wide highway. A few cars faced them, reinforcing how they were going the wrong way.

"Do you see anyone?" He took a chance going in blind, but if they stuck around until they saw the Predator again, they'd risk also being seen in return. If the drone was searching for them a mile or two away, they'd be hard to spot. Plus, the highway was lined with tall trees, giving them a bit more cover.

"Not yet," she said while looking all around. "My god, these windows are so small. I can barely see out the back and sides."

"Let's keep notes," he deadpanned, "so we can tell the salesman when we bring this back to the dealership."

"Agreed," she said distractedly, continuing her search.

He kept his eyes on the road as the speedometer went beyond 100 miles per hour. There weren't a lot of abandoned cars on the highway, and they were easy to avoid.

The little Cessna 172 burned on the same highway a couple of miles back, and the men of the Piper Cherokee were probably spread out, still looking for them. The Predator drone was the only threat he had to worry about right now, however, because it could catch up to them.

The interstate went into a long, sweeping right turn, and he took it at fighter-pilot speed. He stayed toward the inside median because the cars had predictably stacked up on the outer edge of the curve. The motor purred like a champ, and the tires held the road with no slipping or squealing, suggesting there was a lot more power left under the hood.

As the highway straightened out again, the number of wrecked cars grew a bit. They'd come to a rest in all different lanes, and on the shoulders, which required him to slow down and weave through. A few miles later, he had to slam on the brakes in order to fit between a semi-truck and the barrier along the median.

"We better not hit too many of those," he suggested. The other side of the highway was going into downtown Manhattan, and it had been stopped at what would have been rush hour on a Monday morning. It was choked solid with wrecked cars. Their side, going out of the city, was all right, but they still had twenty miles to go.

Ted shifted through the gears back to a hundred, but Emily pointed ahead. "Toll booth!"

He cruised into the toll plaza and went for the express lanes, which was one of the few without at least some cars facing them.

"Piece of cake," he said, keeping his voice even and calm as he gunned the motor again.

"Yeah, well, we'll see," Emily replied.

They'd gone through the toll plaza with no issues, but once they got back up to speed, the interstate left the trees and houses and went into a cleared area. The twists of the highway made it hard to see how close they were to the Newark airport.

Now he knew.

The edge of the property was next to the highway.

"I hope you have your seatbelt on," he said without a hint of humor.

St. Louis, MO

Tabby's eyes were drawn to the floating white drone hovering in the middle of the street. It was likely the same one she'd watched float by at the other end of the alley, but it had come around the building to this side.

"Hide!" she ordered.

They all piled behind a couple of garbage cans, but when she realized there wasn't enough room, she pulled Donovan away from the scrum. "C'mon. We'll go over here."

The two of them hastened to the front edge of a dumpster. Tabby didn't worry about what was inside, she just hopped up and pulled herself over the lip. Donovan followed her lead after chucking his shotgun in ahead of him.

"Oof," he gasped when he landed on the full trash bags.

The lid was propped all the way open, so it leaned against the wall of the building. There wasn't time to pull it shut.

"Shush," she ordered.

The two of them creeped down into the trash, trying to put something between them and the probe.

"Is it coming?" he asked after a short time.

"Quiet!" she whispered.

The machine was close. The whirring of its blades suggested it was at the end of the alley, but it had paused. The MSD truck was parked at the other end. Was that enough to get its attention?

It continued to hover nearby for ten or fifteen seconds. Tabby held her breath, mostly because of the stench inside the dumpster. However, she froze her entire body when the fan wash came into the trash with her.

The machine went by like it had been lit on fire.

Almost immediately, someone called her name at a little more than a whisper. "Tabby!"

She stuck her head up. The drone was almost at the sewer truck.

"Tabby!" the voice repeated.

It was Peter. He'd come out from his hiding place and pointed at Vinny and Gus. They'd taken off to cross the next street.

She turned again to see the drone, but it was now on the other side of the truck, probably running the plates on her car.

"Dammit. We've got to run." She turned to Donovan. "Let's get out."

He didn't argue. The boy hopped out of the stinky dumpster and immediately took off after the two men. Peter and Audrey ran with him, but lagged behind, as if to give her time to catch up. She climbed out, but couldn't resist wiping her legs and arms, sure some trash was stuck to her. A couple of seconds later, she checked one more time for the drone, then sprinted after her young friends.

"Are they still going to the TV station?" she asked when she almost caught up.

Peter waved her on. "Yeah, they said it's on the next block."

Vinny and Gus ran diagonal to the alley, so the drone was no longer in their line of sight. That solved their immediate problem, but as they went along the wide downtown avenue, they were visible for a quarter of a mile in each direction.

The kids made like they were going to pause at a parked car along the side of the street, so she urged them on. "Keep going! Don't stop."

The four of them ran around a corner and along an even wider avenue. This one was miles long; they could be seen from any point along the length of it. However, they ran next to the cars in the parking lane to make themselves harder to spot.

As promised, the station was on the next block. They had to cross one more street before running up to the glass front doors. Vinny waved them in, the automatic doors opening for them.

"Thanks," she huffed.

"Welcome," the sanitation worker replied with a tip of his Blues hat.

Gus was already inside, hunched over like he'd run himself out of oxygen. She was winded, too, but not to such an extent. The two boys appeared fine, but Audrey seemed as exhausted as the old man.

"You okay?" she asked the girl. "You need your meds?"

"I'm fine," Audrey replied.

"Anyone know where to go?" she asked.

Vinny pointed the way. "When we did our work, we went down this hallway, past the sound booth."

It was unnaturally quiet in the building, though there was a low hissing sound coming out of speakers hung from several of the walls, like they were supposed to be broadcasting but no one was at the microphone.

Vinny and Gus went into the cheery hallway filled with broadcasting awards and posters of famous events in the city's history. She hardly recognized any of them, except for the giant poster of the Stanley Cup, which the Blues had recently won. Hockey wasn't her thing, but Dad had repeatedly told her about it the past few weeks.

Vinny touched the poster of the trophy, then pointed through tall glass windows to a big room with numerous cameras angled toward a desk with the number 5 on the wall behind it. "Right in there."

Tabby pushed through the double-doors, glad they were unlocked. She strode up to the desk but paused when two sets of clothes caught her eye. The news anchors had been in the chairs behind the desk, like they'd been live on the air when things happened.

She continued marching forward and went to the set of clothing for a woman. Tabby pulled the small lapel microphone out of the blouse, then pushed the rest of the ensemble onto the floor.

"Hello? Is this thing on?"

"I hear you!" Audrey shouted. "Your voice is coming through the speakers outside."

Tabby looked at the big camera pointed at her. She thought of how far she'd come since missing that elevator in the mine shaft. Would

Mom and Dad see her on television? Were they watching safely in some motel outside the disaster cordon? She had to believe they were.

"Say something," Peter cajoled.

"Here we go..." she exhaled.

SIXTEEN

Poor Sisters Convent, Oakville, MO

Sister Rose sat in the front seat of the van, unsure what to do. The floating machine had asked for her name, but she didn't feel comfortable interacting with such an unusual piece of technology. It could be dangerous.

"Are people still alive?" she asked it. "Can we get to safety?" Tabby had been convinced help was out there and took off to go find it, but Rose didn't believe it was true. Couldn't believe it. Now there was potentially a second source who could confirm it.

"Please state your name," the machine requested.

Rose glanced over at Deogee. She had her head cocked to one side with an ear perked up.

The dog seemed to be confused as to whether this was a threat or not.

"I'm Sister Rose," she said in a mouse-like squeak.

"Please increase volume when speaking."

It was the oddest feeling for Rose. It was like talking to the order-takers in a fast-food drive-through, but this time, there was no human around. Was it really a computer or were people somewhere nearby? She had to know.

"Can you tell me where you are?" she asked it.

"This is the Poor Sisters Convent, in Oakville, Missouri." The machine gave her the address and included what it called GPS coordinates. It appeared to be very thorough about listing every detail for her location. She figured out during this data dump the white copter was responding with precision to the question she'd asked.

"Please state your name," the computer said in the same patient tone as before.

"Sister Rose. My given name is Becky Hatcher. I'm a novitiate nun in the convent. Who are you?" She kept her voice pleasant and courteous. Whatever it was, it would do no good to be rude to it or whoever controlled it.

"Please confirm social security number," the box requested.

She hesitated for twenty or thirty seconds because she'd always been taught not to give out that information for anyone unless you were sure it wouldn't be used for identity theft. This strange device could be controlled by criminals.

"I'm afraid I only give that out over the phone."

The floating box spun around, but the orb underneath remained stationary from her perspective. It was almost impossible to read the mood of the little aircraft, but she imagined it was upset with her.

"This area has been designated as inhospitable due to an industrial accident. Social security ident requested to ensure proper dispatch of emergency services extraction vehicle. Please confirm social security number to ensure speedy recovery."

The voice showed no signs of impatience or anxiety, but she began to feel both. If someone was coming to rescue her, that would be wonderful, but, for some reason, talking to the computer woman didn't make her feel comfortable about it.

Deogee seemed to pick up on her emotions; she got up on her seat and walked in a circle. Then she sat on her haunches while facing the menacing box floating outside.

With great reluctance, she gave her social to the computer woman. No matter how bad she felt about it, she wanted to be totally sure rescuers could find her and the nice dog. She'd also tell them about the other dogs nearby. Maybe now she didn't need to go to the pet store to buy food for them, if rescue was close.

"How long will I have to wait?"

"Computing travel time... Approximately seven minutes."

"Wow! Okay. I need to get my stuff. Thank you so much for telling me."

"The St. Louis County Police Department thanks you for your cooperation."

She breathed out a sigh of relief. If it would have told her up front it was with the police, she wouldn't have had so much trepidation about it.

"You're welcome."

Rose pulled the keys out of the ignition, feeling a lot better about the exchange. The little drone rose in the air and waited at the edge of the parking lot. She thought there was a new window open on the side of the little machine's frame, but it was hard to be sure in the daylight. It almost looked like a little beam of red light pointed at the convent's front door.

"Sorry, Deogee. We'll get food for you when we get to the police station."

She opened the door to get out, but the hound didn't move. It sat with teeth bared and stared at the white box.

"Oh, you. No need to be worried. It's with the authorities. We're saved!"

Newark, NJ

Ted's stomach twirled a few times as he figured out how exposed they were.

"Lincoln Tunnel, ten miles!" Emily pointed at the green sign above the eastbound lanes as they raced along the edge of the airport. He got a better look at the dozens of commercial jets, mostly A380s and 777s, taxiing back and forth, as well as scores of military recon drones lined up in one stretch of tarmac.

"Damn, Emily, this looks like an invasion," he blurted as he kept the car between the white lines.

"And look at those shipping containers," Emily remarked, "over at the port."

Beyond the wide-open expanse of runways and taxiways, huge cranes lifted tractor-trailer-sized shipping containers off a massive ship stacked high with them. The level of activity at the docks matched the ant-like fervor at the airport.

Ted barely had time to see where she'd pointed because he had to slow and dodge a wrecked fuel truck. He locked his elbows and jammed on the brakes.

"Hang on!" he croaked.

It wasn't only a wrecked truck, but a medium-sized jet had come down, clipped vehicles on the highway, then crashed into a field. The stretch of highway was the start of the debris field.

Metal and rock clattered off the undercarriage as he did sixty through a patch of charred pavement. If they caught some bad luck and blew a tire, they'd have to stop on the exposed stretch of highway. They'd be visible to the entire airport.

Ted went a little slower toward the far edge of the mess, hoping they'd get through. A metal bar made a pair of loud thumps as the tires struck it, but then it went silent. After a few tense moments waiting to see if they still had tire pressure, he kicked the Camaro in the gut to get it back up to escape velocity.

The highway turned north, away from the airport.

"We're up to one-fifty," he announced proudly. Ted checked in the rearview mirror, but the small windows and bad angles didn't allow him to keep tabs on the airport. "You tell me if anything is following us. They'll never catch us on the ground, but that Predator is still out there, and there's plenty more at the airport."

He wondered how many ships were behind those already dockside. Did the US Navy know these were converging on the coastline before the event struck yesterday? How many people could fit on a ship? How did they survive whatever death ray killed everyone else?

If an enemy wanted to come to America, Newark was a good place to start. Everything was free for the taking. Just as he and Emily were scavenging their way up the coast of the northeast, any invading force would find lots of goodies ripe for the plucking. Maybe the bad guys here were preparing transport for the follow-on forces waiting at airports elsewhere in the world.

If any of the intel spooks had survived on Air Force Two, they'd have a field day with this.

There was nothing but questions for him as his Camaro thundered along the wide-open highway. The needle nudged higher, toward one-sixty, but the steering wheel started to vibrate because of the poor surface conditions.

"I see aircraft back there," Emily gulped. "At least two."

"How far?"

She studied the sky for a few seconds. "They're still by the airport."

He thought about their situation as a classic math word problem. How long would it take to go less than ten miles while doing 160 miles per hour? The solution was ever-changing since he ticked off another mile every forty seconds.

"We can make it," he said hesitantly. It wasn't that he was being wishy-washy, but there were more wrecked cars up ahead.

"Okay, now they're definitely coming our way." Emily had her face up against the glass of her window as she surveyed the skies behind them.

"They can't launch at us," he said with another dose of barely-contained hesitation. They probably would if they knew Emily was in the car, but not for two joy-riding nuts. Missiles were expensive.

The Camaro sounded happy to be going fast, and it coaxed him to try for even more speed. He held the wheel as tight as he could while they sped across a long, curving bridge over a river. The sweeping turn collected the abandoned cars in the far lanes, so he was able to maintain his speed until he was across. Then the highway turned to the left, and more junk cars were in his lanes.

"Five miles!" Emily pointed to the road sign.

"Madam President, hold on. It's going to get bumpy."

Ted feathered the brakes to take off some speed, then he switched lanes to avoid a T-bone collision with a school bus. As he came around the back bumper, he had to brake again; a second bus was behind the first.

"That way!" Emily pointed to the right shoulder, by a concrete barrier, because it was the only lane open. The buses must have turned sideways and caught other vehicles.

He jumped in his seat when the tires rubbed up against the median wall.

"One more deduction," Emily remarked with dark humor.

His heart pounded in his chest with the same ferocity he'd experienced on his first deployment. People depended on him to do a good job and pull through this.

"I'm getting the job," Ted reassured her. He exhaled a deep breath because he'd been holding it since before the bus wreck.

She pointed to another overhead sign that alerted drivers of the need to be in the right lane to get to the Lincoln Tunnel.

"C'mon," she encouraged him, "you'll get us there."

They blew through another toll booth, then went up and onto a flyover ramp. For a few moments, they had a front-row view of the mega-fire burning to the north. It was only a few miles away. So close they could smell it.

"Glad we aren't going that way," he said, keeping his eyes on the road.

The curved ramp took them off the first highway and onto one heading directly for the city. Many of the cars had rolled into the wall, making it easier for them to use the cleared inside lane, but once the highway straightened out, it became more difficult to see a path through the wrecks. Both directions of roadway were stuffed with abandoned vehicles.

"We aren't stopping," he deadpanned.

Ahead, the skyscrapers of New York City beckoned them from three or four miles away. However, as they headed due east through the ever-narrowing gaps in the stalled traffic, Ted had to keep dropping speed. It gave the enemy a chance to close the distance.

Emily tapped on her window with a fingernail. "The planes are coming."

Amarillo, TX

When Brent got inside the trailer, he immediately found Trish on the floor next to the kitchen table. Her phone was crushed on the linoleum next to her, and she'd been crying.

"Are you okay?" he asked after he'd rushed over to her.

"She's fine, pops," Curtis assured him. "Why would we hurt someone we wanted to treat real nice? We need her."

Trish smiled weakly. She was normally a cocky, self-sure woman, but a few punches had beat her down. Still, there was fire behind those eyes, like she was ready to get even.

He tried to reason with them. "Boys, this is ridiculous. The whole world has gone to shit. People have disappeared. You're free of your old lives. You don't have to be criminals."

Curtis strode into the kitchen with a shotgun over his shoulder. It was one from the armory, which meant the men he'd come with had truly betrayed him. The young man moved a chair across the floor so he could look directly at him and Trish. "I'll never be free, pops, don't you get it? No? Try this on for size..."

He threw the gun on the wooden table, then sat down.

"I got caught dealing last year. Small-time stuff, no big deal. It was in some West Texas town I don't even remember. As I'm sitting in the police cruiser, some asshole in a suit comes up to me and says I work for him now. I gave him the finger, but he opened the door in front of the deputy, pulled me out, and held a gun to my head."

Brent shifted uncomfortably on his sore knees.

"Are you getting the point?" Curtis said with exasperation. "The guy whispered in my ear, giving me marching orders for his operation. He said if I didn't follow them to the letter, he was going to kill my whole family. The officer told him my home address, as a way to let me know he had me by the balls."

Curtis touched his bandana. "If I cross them in any way, I'm screwed big time. So, I figure it's better to embrace my job and survive this thing as top dog, you know?"

Brent was caught in a crouch, but he had to stand up to relieve the pressure on his legs. He groaned on his way up.

"You need help, pops. Why are you even here?" Curtis pointed to Brent's legs. "We'll let you go if you simply walk away."

That made some of the other prisoners mumble in disagreement.

"No, it's fine," Curtis assured them. "He's one guy, and we'll send him packing with a butter knife for a weapon. No one has to get hurt over this girl."

Brent shook his head in disappointment. "Would you get out of your arrangement with those assholes if you could?"

Curtis nodded. "Of course, but I can't."

"You can," Brent insisted. "Everyone is gone. Don't you get it? The top level of the prison was cleared out. The surrounding towns are empty. Amarillo and Austin aren't picking up their phones. No one is on any of the radio stations. The world has gone quiet."

Curtis squinted at him. "Can you prove to me all the cartels are gone?"

He shrugged. "How the hell should I know? But I'd bet anything the dickhead threatening you is gone. Everyone in Texas is apparently...gone."

The man seemed to think about it.

"Naw, I ain't falling for that. I'm—" Curtis didn't get a chance to finish. Paul put a pistol on Curtis's cheek, which caused a chain reaction of gun pointing throughout the rest of the prisoners.

Brent's six friends hadn't abandoned him after all, but everyone was in danger of being killed.

"Don't shoot!" he yelled.

SEVENTEEN

West Portal, Lincoln Tunnel, NJ

"I can see a problem developing," Ted remarked as the traffic continued to get thicker. He wasn't able to do more than fifty and had to brake and swerve every few seconds, though they were still moving forward.

"Let me guess this one. They know where we are and where we're going." Emily remained fixated out her window.

They were close to the tunnel now. To his right, through the trees and brick homes of this New Jersey neighborhood, the highway wrapped around in a spiral as it went down into the tunnel entrance.

"You're pretty smart, for a politician," he mused.

"Well, pilot, what are you going to do now?"

There was no time to think of elaborate schemes. In his view, there was only one viable way to end this before they would be forced to stop anyway.

Ted scraped against a parked car, startling himself in the process. When he gave it some more gas, he glanced over to Emily. "Hold onto your gun."

She turned and held onto her rifle, then he steered the expensive Camaro to the right—toward the median. He stood on the brakes to remove some of the danger, but he also jammed the wheel so the car would spin around next to the barrier. It reminded him of wiping out on a kid's bike.

"Whoa!" Emily screeched.

The Camaro was in-line with the rest of the traffic, so it wouldn't stick out.

They'd stopped near an overpass. Below him, to the left and right, the tree-lined residential streets offered more anonymity.

"Go! Get below this bridge and then we'll go from there." Ted scrambled to grab his gun and backpack, then he struggled to force his door open. It opened about a foot, then banged into the wall.

"Take a deep breath, dumbass," he said to himself. After shutting the door, he slid across the center console and hurried out Emily's door. He closed that too as another way to blend the car back into traffic. An open door would be a giveaway that someone had used it after the attack on America.

She was already running over the side of the highway and down the embankment.

The engine whine of multiple drones carried across the quiet landscape. One of them came from behind, like it had finally caught up to them. Its distinctive wing configuration and weapons payload lined up along the crowded highway.

Orange fire spurted from underneath the bird, signaling the launch of a missile.

"Dive!" Ted dove behind a nearby truck, then rolled toward the slope where Emily had gone.

The screaming hiss of missile thrust whipped by the instant before an explosion. A blast of heat washed over him as he tumbled down the hill and small pieces of metal rained all around. He came to a stop near the bottom, and looked up toward the highway—

A flaming four-door sedan rolled down the hill.

"Jump!" Emily shouted from somewhere far away.

The car bounced left and right, so it was hard to pick a side. In the end, he guessed and stumbled to his right to get out of its way.

The wreck bounced by, hitting a tree trunk close to where he'd been standing.

Ted fell to the ground panting after the quick bursts of energy.

"We have to keep going!" Emily said, again from somewhere far away. No, she was close... He saw her twenty feet from him. The problem was in his head. His ears rang from the concussive blast, muffling the sounds.

"To the tunnel!" he said, as if remembering why he'd abandoned the car.

Somehow, he still had his pack in his hands, so he slung it over both shoulders and started to run along the street that ran under the highway. When they'd gone about a quarter of a mile, he turned back to see where they'd come from.

Emily stopped with him. "Do you think they'll give up?"

"No," he said without a pause. "I'm sure they saw us escape. Our only hope now is that they don't see us go into the tunnel."

He pulled at her hand to keep her on the move.

By the time they'd gotten within sight of the tunnel entrance, there were three Predator drones cutting across the sky above them. If they were all armed, it meant there were five Hellfire missiles with the names Ted and Emily on them.

"I see the way down," he whispered. "We go through those trees, stay under that billboard, then climb down the rock wall." The tunnel entrance was basically a long ramp that went into the earth. Three individual tubes carried two lanes of traffic each, and it appeared as if the two tunnels on the right were going into the city

235

because they were stuffed with cars and trucks. The one on the left must have been coming out of New York, because there wasn't a car on it.

She whispered back, "We'll be exposed. Are you sure? Maybe we can wait now? Until dark?"

"Nah. Nighttime is still hours away. They used an expensive missile on our car. They can't have missed us tumbling down that hill. I'd bet anything they're going to send in ground forces to investigate."

Emily rubbed her neck. "I'm going back to the gym after this. I should have after running that half-marathon, but politicking has made me soft."

He didn't think that was true at all. She might have been petite, but she wasn't weak or out of shape. She'd been keeping up with him on their journey like a boss. It wasn't by chance he'd been looking at her legs when they were back on Air Force Two...

"Get a grip," he ordered himself. It wasn't the time to be checking out the President of the United States. Not now, not ever.

"Move out," he ordered.

They hopped a small black fence, then climbed over the edge of the rock wall marking the border of the ramp area going down toward the tunnels. He hopped onto a small ledge, then waited for her to do the same.

"I hear them," she said with rising panic.

"Me, too," he admitted. "Don't stop."

The next leg was a drop of about ten feet to the asphalt below. He first chucked his backpack down, then hung off the ledge to let himself fall after it. When he hit the ground, he scooped up his bag and waited for her.

She dropped down right as he looked up. Emily stuck the landing but stumbled back a few steps as she struggled to gain her balance. That sent her right into his arms.

"Got ya!" he whooped in triumph. They'd come down next to the empty tunnel going out of the city, which was the one he'd wanted, but before she could turn around or say thank you, he shoved her hard toward the tunnel entrance before them.

Outside, the growl of a missile launch suggested they were out of time.

"Run!" His voice echoed in the tunnel.

St. Louis, MO

"My name is Tabitha Breeze. I'm from Bonne Terre, Missouri. I survived the poison gas with three students from Seckman High School." She relayed all the names, but also had Peter, Audrey, and Donovan stand next to her at the desk. "We are here in the studios of Channel 5. Please help us evacuate."

She looked around, not sure what to add.

"There are also a couple of sanitation workers." She looked at Gus and Vinny. "Would you two like to say a few words?"

Both men crowded into the shot. Gus stated his name and occupation with the sewer company, but his message was more personal. "MJ, if you're still alive, I'll be here waiting for you."

The old man looked to his partner. Vinny turned to the camera, gave his name and address, then seemed at a loss for what to say next.

She leaned his way. "You don't have to say anything more."

"I know," he agreed, "but I guess I want to say something to my parents. If you get this broadcast, I'm sorry for saying those mean things before I left..."

The air became stale as they all stared vacantly into the camera. Tabby imagined they'd found a method of rescue, but it was going to take time before someone saw the message and came to get them. It was no different than stuffing a letter in a bottle and throwing it in the ocean.

What started with so much hope and excitement now ended with uncertainty.

Vinny and Gus walked away from the news desk, but the kids stayed with her.

"We must look pretty badass," Peter remarked, holding his shotgun for the camera and bending awkwardly at the waist to show off his police utility belt.

Tabby was horrified. She faced the camera again, too. "I didn't give guns to the children. We found these at an empty police station. I promise we'll give them back as soon as we find someone in charge, which I hope is soon..."

Donovan teared up.

"What is it, D?" she asked with sympathy.

He stood up and moved out of the frame of the camera. She unclipped the mic and followed.

"This is pointless. Our parents are all dead—"

"Not mine," she interjected.

"Fine. Whatever. *My* parents are dead. We saw them at my house. What am I supposed to do? I don't even know if any of my relatives are alive. Should I go look for them?"

"No!" she answered. Her job was to keep them together until they found the authorities. They had to be getting close to that. "Well, I mean, not yet. Once this message gets to whoever is watching the news, we'll be rescued. Those are the people who will help you find your family again."

He sniffled but seemed content.

She, however, became aware of Gus looking at her from across the studio. He'd gotten out another cigarette and tugged at it furiously, as if thinking hard about his next move.

After what she'd said on camera about the guns, it seemed hypocritical to wish she'd brought her shotgun, but the creepy vibe wouldn't go away. She secretly enjoyed the rub of the pistol against the small of her back. It gave her comfort to know it was there, and it maintained her feeling of being in charge.

"Gather up, guys," she said to the kids. "We're going to wait in the front lobby so we can see when help is coming." She thought it would also be a good place to go in case they needed to get away from Gus.

The gray-haired man continued to focus his eyes on her, but she ignored him as she walked by. Tabby glanced over her shoulder as she exited the studio to make sure the kids followed.

"Shit," she muttered. The guy had moved next to the doorway, probably to watch her walk away, creeper style.

Tabby's nerves were on an electricity-fueled edge because she wanted to be anywhere but there. If she could get her friends gathered, maybe they could slip away. They'd jump out when help arrived...

Donovan and Audrey came through the doorway after her, but Peter lagged behind like he owned the place. He'd hefted the shotgun, so it balanced on his right shoulder. It was ripe for plucking...

Peter, you fool.

She opened her mouth to say something, but it was already too late.

Gus hit Peter's shotgun barrel, which popped *Audrey Two* up and out of the boy's hand. Because he didn't have a good grip, it rolled over his back, right into Gus's arms.

"What the hell, man!" the boy screamed in agony.

Tabby fumbled for her pistol a moment after Gus captured the gun. Peter had fallen to one side, away from Gus, as if dodging an attack. Audrey and Donovan barely looked back because they didn't understand what had happened.

"Move!" she shouted.

The kids scrambled in multiple directions, making it hard for her to properly aim the pistol. Gus wasn't encumbered by such worries. He brought the shotgun to bear on the first person he could.

Tabby had the advantage. Her pistol was at the ready and aimed at the filthy nametag of the sanitation worker, even as his shotgun came up.

All she had to do was pull the trigger.

EIGHTEEN

Newark, NJ

"Help!" Kyla screamed.

The helicopter banked in a tight left turn, as if the pilot wanted to reverse course the second he saw the explosion at the overpass. The g-forces kept her pinned to the outside skin of the aircraft, and the tether was the only thing keeping her from falling to the houses below.

She noticed a second plane gliding down onto the highway, but the banked turn soon made her lose track of it.

"Hang on," Meechum said calmly over the headset.

She didn't have much choice, but as the Skyhawk straightened its flight path, she managed to pull herself along the cord. Kyla struggled to reach the door handhold.

"We going back out to sea?" Meechum asked the pilot.

Kyla didn't care in the least about that; she only wanted some help climbing back in. However, rather than flap in the wind waiting, she continued her efforts to find that handhold. The second she found it, Kyla pulled herself onto the cargo hold floor.

Meechum grabbed her by the shoulders and pulled her away from the door. "Girl, you almost did a no-chute para-jump. That's hardcore!"

She didn't feel like it was worthy of such praise. The helicopter bumped up and down as they hit some turbulence, which made them both grab onto the back row of seats. She was so scared she laughed maniacally. "I think I'm going to puke!"

"Not on me, dudette! Just don't let go, okay?"

Kyla and Meechum got in their seats and buckled in. Almost immediately after making the seatbelt click, the pilot banked them again, but she was ready for it.

A voice interrupted her headset. "Looks like an old-model Predator drone is taking off from the Newark Airport."

She and Meechum shared concerned looks.

"We have another drone between us and the ocean. It was already in the air." The pilot angled the helicopter away from the coast and toward Staten Island. "I'm going to see if I can get around it."

Kyla was already nervous to the point of throwing up, but the rollercoaster ups and downs almost brought up her breakfast. The large earmuff headphones blocked out most of the sound, but there were buzzing alarms up by the pilot she heard with near-perfect clarity. She didn't know what they were for, but it had to be related to the air pursuit closing in on them.

She found it helped when she focused herself out the side door, down to the homes and streets below. As she looked out on the urban sprawl, New York City and the surrounding rivers came into view. Closer, a bit to the north of Staten Island, she caught sight of the Newark Airport as well as a bunch of huge ships actively unloading shipping containers at a port facility already filled with them.

"Just breathe," she reassured herself. "That's how you get through this."

Meechum, for once, looked almost as uncomfortable as her. "How are you doing?" she asked the Marine.

The blonde-haired woman glanced sideways at her, almost to the point of being offended, but then she relented a bit. "I hate flying!"

"Really? I didn't think anything could get you down. Hell, you were sitting on the edge a second ago!" She didn't tell the woman she'd inspired her to do the same.

Meechum grinned. "I hate not being in control, that's all."

Kyla had spent her life leaving the control to someone else. Working for the Navy was all about following orders and doing as she was told, even if she wasn't formally in a uniform. Nothing happened without massive packets of orders and guidelines.

The pilot drove them in wild circles for a couple of minutes before he came back on the intercom. "I can't get around these bastards. I think they're trying to box us in, so we're forced to land close to the airport. I don't think Captain Van Nuys would approve of that."

Meechum spoke to the pilot. "Can you put us down at Battery Park? We can finish our mission while also distracting the enemy from you. Maybe that will help you get away."

"Seriously? You want me to put you in the city?"

"Yeah," Kyla agreed, "are you sure that's wise?"

The Marine nodded. "I was given a mission to investigate New York. We'll either find some people there, or we won't. Either way, I can go back to the ship and give Carthager some actionable intel he can then give to the captain."

"Damn," Kyla said quietly.

The bottom dropped out as the pilot shredded some more altitude, then the scenery outside turned to all water. They were now south of the city, heading toward the blocky skyline.

"I'll go with you," Kyla added, surprised to hear herself say it. Getting out wasn't what she had in mind when she climbed aboard earlier, but she was committed to staying with her new friend.

The pilot worked the commands and spoke to someone on a different channel. A minute later, he reported to Meechum. "The JFK has cleared you to hop out. I'll drop you at Battery Park, like you requested. Up ahead."

Meechum held the mic to her face. "You're coming back for us, right?"

"Affirmative. I don't know if I can shake those guys, but I'm going to try."

She had no idea how fast the helicopter could go, but it seemed like the pilot was pushing it to the limit. They passed over more of the giant ships stacked with containers, and they went by another series of docks with massive cranes designed to pull the containers off the deck. They also passed the Statue of Liberty, which she saw from a couple of hundred feet away, outside her door.

And the colossal fire was always there, with a smoke plume rising to the heavens.

"This is crazy," she said to herself, forgetting Meechum could hear her.

"I'll take care of you, dudette. Don't get scared on me, okay?"

"Oh, I'm scared, but I'll get over it. What's going to happen to the pilot? Won't they shoot him down?"

Meechum shrugged. "You know these Navy jocks. They like to be the hero."

The pilot laughed. "If they force me down, it's better if you two aren't on board. Get to Central Park. If I get clear, I'll come back later, I promise. I'll pick you up there."

Kyla didn't like the plan at all, but she still knew enough not to tell military people how to do their jobs.

"Roger that," she said at the same time as Meechum.

The other woman smiled at her. "You're getting the hang of this."

Then the Marine picked up her rifle.

Lincoln Tunnel, NY

Ted and Emily didn't stick around the exit to see where the Hellfire missile landed. They ran into the well-lit automotive tunnel and didn't slow until they went around a curve. During the entire run, he'd imagined the missile skipping off the pavement as it cruised by them. However, that was the cartoon version. In the real world, it would explode on impact and kill them from a distance because there was nowhere else for the blast and shrapnel to go.

When they came to an abandoned taxi, he checked the door and then climbed inside. "We. Have. Keys." His breathing was labored from the sprint.

Emily got in, huffing the same way. "Did they shoot at us?"

The answer made all the difference. If they'd been the target, it meant someone knew they were in the tunnel. If the target was something else, like their wrecked Camaro, it could mean they'd escaped.

"I'm not even going to guess. Either way, we have to keep moving."

He tried to start the motor, but realized the key was already turned. The engine had idled itself out of fuel.

"Damn! We need a different car. A stick!"

They both got out and trotted fifty yards to the next vehicle. That one was an automatic, too, and it was also out of gas. They tried two more before finding an old stick shift.

"Eesh, this thing is a shit-barn," he remarked. The make and model were unknown, but it reminded him of an old Yugo. It was small and ugly, but it did start.

Their bag and guns filled up the back seat.

As he got it going, the little fender rubbed against the side wall of the tunnel, but he backed it off, then did a ten-point U-turn to get them pointed back toward New York City.

Emily spoke as he made his maneuver. "It's nice we keep finding cars and planes to borrow. We should put notes in each one we use. An IOU, if you will."

"Yeah," he mused, "we should go to the coin factory and make up your presidential challenge coin." He tapped his pocket where he still had the one Ramirez had given him. "We could drop a coin in each one."

Ted got the Yugo clone to about thirty-five miles per hour.

Emily tapped her nails against the wood-grained glove box. "Do you really think they want us dead? I mean, not us as important government employees, but as generic American citizens. It seems like they aren't very discerning in who they kill."

"It seems that way." He stole a glance at her. She still wore the torn blouse material over her nose and mouth as part of their disguise. His was gone, though it was hard to remember where he'd lost it. Probably when he dove away from the Camaro and fell down that hill. "This is almost certainly an invasion, Emily, and the bad thing is there are no war correspondents left alive to report it."

"Our bases around the world know about it. Air Force Two told them while we were airborne. We just have to wait until they come home and start fighting back."

"Maybe," he said with great distraction. Driving in the arched tunnel reminded him of going through a long public bathroom. Large, white tiles covered every inch of the walls, archway, and ceiling. The faint scent of sewage seemed to hang on the air. It went in a perfectly straight line for almost a mile with few abandoned cars, but there was a jam up ahead.

Several cars had come to a rest in the sideways position, blocking those behind it. He guessed he might be able to bully the little vehicle through the first couple of cars, but not all of them behind it.

"We've got to ditch our ride, but I can see the light ahead. We're almost home free. The city is right there." Ted shut off the motor.

Emily put one hand on the door handle yet glanced over to him. "Yeah, but are they waiting for us out there?"

That was the million-dollar question.

San Francisco, CA

Dwight followed the footprints up the beach, but the people walked onto a nearby sidewalk, which made it impossible to track them. However, thanks to Poppy's nagging, he couldn't give up and turn around without a brief search, so he trudged on armed only with a wine bottle.

The low foghorn of a ship drifted in from over the harbor. Far out on the water, near the Oakland Bay Bridge, a long ship carried hundreds of shipping containers to an unknown destination. A second one was a few miles behind.

"You can't have mine back!" he yelled.

Poppy gave him a serious glare.

"What? You think they can see me?" He realized what it meant. If there was a ship on the bay, it meant he wasn't alone. The real test was whether they could see him.

"Hey! Wahoo! Hello!" He waved his arms and did his best to jump up and down, though the liquor slowed him. "It's finally happening!"

A man startled him from behind. "Yes, it is."

Dwight spun around. The wine bottle slid out of his hand and shattered on the pavement. "Oh my! You scared the holy bejesus out of me."

"Where have you been?" the man asked.

"I've been walking around the city." He had no intention of giving away his old home in the sub-basement of the skyscraper because he might need it again. "Just now I crawled out of my new shipping container." He looked down. "I don't have a snazzy outfit like yours."

Dwight saw two of the man because his eyes wouldn't focus right. However, when he really put all his energy into the effort, he got a good look at the guy: he was middle-aged, somewhat Asian-looking, and was dressed in a black jumpsuit with black sneakers.

By contrast, Dwight wore faded, dirty blue jeans that were two sizes too big, and a blue shirt that was two sizes too small. The only times he cared about how he looked were in the brief moments between finishing a drinking binge and starting the next one, which was where he was at that moment. "I, uh, have been down on my luck today."

The man nodded. "Some of us have found this city to be full of dangers. Come to the welcome center and we'll get you squared away."

"What? Me?" He was always wary of do-gooders who tried to give him more than a few dollars. Those people who handed him sandwiches or savings bonds were always trying to get him on the right path. All he wanted was more money for the cheapest happy drink he could find.

"Sure! We're all in this together now." There was something about the man's behavior that made Dwight agree to go along with him.

"No, I don't want one of those fancy suits," he whispered to Poppy.

But he kind of did.

NINETEEN

New York City, NY

Ted stood at the edge of the Lincoln Tunnel, in the shadows of the surrounding skyscrapers. The traffic must have been light when the event happened; there was a short line of cars and trucks backed up two or three blocks. However, there were dozens of vehicles at the threshold to the underground highway, as if they'd all come to a stop at the same place when their drivers disappeared.

Emily came up behind him. "We're in midtown Manhattan."

They listened intently for the sound of Predator drones, but he didn't hear anything in the air except for a faraway helicopter.

"You know this area?" he whispered.

She leaned to get a better look outside. "My husband and I used to live here. We talked about it earlier."

"New York is a big city. Are you saying you lived right here?" His sister lived in the city, but far north of Central Park in a place called Pelham Bay. He had no idea what was around this exit tunnel because it was miles from her apartment.

Emily pointed to a connecting avenue. "Yeah, close. I live up by Central Park, which is about ten blocks that way."

As he listened, he considered where they should go. As long as they stayed within the tall skyscraper canyons of the city, the Predator drones would have a hard time tracking them. Even if a drone operator was cocky enough to fly into the area or drop between buildings, they would never be able to make ninety-degree turns, so Ted and Emily could easily evade them. At least, in a perfect world.

"We should go that way." Ted pointed where she'd indicated. "Since you're familiar with the area."

She flung her head back to clear away her bangs. "I'm familiar with the area, but not how things are now. Even seeing these same streets doesn't feel right. The last time I was through this tunnel entrance, cars were stacked up for miles in every direction. Now, everything is stopped. The city is dead. Everyone...is dead."

Ted pulled his rifle over his shoulder and held it in a comfortable two-handed grip. It was the stance soldiers and airmen used when they wanted to convey a sense of wary calm. "We'll run up the ramp and get to your street, then we'll take it slow."

He worried bringing Emily back to her home turf might have been a mistake, especially if her husband was there. It was a fact he'd overlooked until that moment. Still, given the option of walking into strange land or the familiar, he chose the latter.

Emily already had her rifle at the ready.

"Go!" he ordered.

They threaded the needle through the traffic snarl, always with one eye on the surrounding buildings and one ear on the sky. There would probably be no better place to put snipers than at the exits of the bridges and tunnels. Drones could fly above the open waterways bracketing Manhattan, always on the prowl for movement inside the urban core.

Neither spoke when they cleared the vehicles and hopped onto the sidewalk of 10th Avenue. The six-lane road was filled with vehicles all silently facing north. Emily looked at them like they'd soon start moving, but he only saw how exposed they were to overhead surveillance.

"Em," he whispered, "let's keep moving."

Emily looked at him funny. He thought it was because he'd used a nickname for her, but she seemed to snap out of her reverie. "Oh, right. This way." She motioned the same direction the traffic had been flowing.

They ran for several blocks, which gave him time to wonder if he'd offended her. Most of his awareness focused on listening for bad guys, including the whump-whump sound of that big helicopter constantly at the edge of his hearing. However, he also found time to second-guess how he'd addressed his boss.

He followed her until she stopped at a street corner.

"Look," she exclaimed.

All concerns about addressing a superior slipped away as he came up beside her. A long line of blue and gray school uniforms littered the sidewalk for fifty yards. Little pairs of pants were mostly in one row, while girls' jumpers were in the other one.

Without thinking, he held out his arms and she put her head on his chest. The position left him looking at the fallen children, but he didn't get choked up like she did. He'd grieved yesterday when those tiny soccer uniforms blew over the highway. Today, he was going to help his friend.

Emily didn't take long. She'd pulled down her face mask and wiped her nose in an unflattering way, but then she stepped back from him. "I'm sorry. I know I've got to be stronger about scenes like this. I'm not being very presidential."

"It's all right. I'm not going to lie to you, ma'am, but I saw something like this yesterday and it ripped out a piece of my soul. Since then,

I've been keeping myself sane by swearing I'm going to get the bastards who did this. Someone, maybe the people driving those drones, used a new weapon on us." He pointed to the uniforms. "These pour souls are counting on us to hold it together and fight back."

She fixed her face mask. He got the sense she did it to hide her embarrassed expression.

"Emily, listen to me. I know this is horrible, but it's good you saw it now. It's going to make you stronger..." He thought it over for a few seconds. "This is total war on a scale beyond anything in human history. If we don't shed tears for this disaster, we don't deserve to be called humans at all. No one on Earth would see this as a weakness, president or not."

The expression behind the mask flickered happiness for a moment. "Thanks, Ted. I needed to hear that." She turned toward the school uniforms and spoke in a respectful voice. "I'm sorry, boys and girls. I'm sorry, everyone. It's like he said: we're going to get the bastards who did this to you."

Without waiting for him, she strode out into the street to go to the next block over.

He followed, sure the helicopter rotor noises had gotten louder.

St. Louis, MO

Tabby's knees wobbled as she faced the shotgun, but the barrel wasn't pointed at her. Gus had it aimed at Peter.

"No! Don't shoot! Please!" She still had her gun aimed at him, but she made a split-second judgment not to shoot it. Even if she hit the guy, it seemed likely he would also fire his shotgun, and one of her kids would be dead.

The old man seemed like he might pull the trigger anyway, which led her to put more pressure on her own, but Gus took his eyes off the boy and glanced over to her. "Lower your gun and I don't have to hurt anyone."

"Why are you doing this? Are you with them?" She tilted her head toward the Arch, hoping he understood what she meant.

"Hell no. Those people killed my friends in the department. I want nothing to do with them, except to take this here gun down there and blow them away."

Tabby's arms wanted to shake as she held the gun with both hands. Audrey and Donovan had guns, too, though they were already through the door, so they were out of Gus's sight. Audrey looked like she might come back in, but Tabby didn't want to escalate the standoff, so she stood inside the frame to block her.

"You could have just asked," she stammered.

Vinny stood off to the side of Gus. "Come on, guys. We're all friends, right?"

"Vin, get her gun. Get all the guns. We're going to fight back."

The young guy didn't move, which made her realize how fast she'd been put in the position to use her pistol. Within the space of seconds, two men threatened to disarm and do her harm. The gun was the only thing preventing that from happening.

"No," she said dryly. "Take Peter's shotgun if you must, but we're not giving up any of the others. I need them to keep the kids safe." If he didn't see the logic of why, then there was no reasoning with him.

265

Gus aimed square at Peter's face. "I don't want to hurt anyone, least of all a kid, but we need those guns and we're going to get them."

Vinny sidestepped to within a few feet of his co-worker. "Gus, I don't want to hurt them. Let's take the one shotgun and call it good." He looked at Tabby as if to say *Sorry, I don't want to be a part of this.*

Gus held the shotgun steady, but then he looked beyond Tabby, through the door. "Oh, crap, they're already here."

A woman's computerized voice interrupted. "Please state your name."

Tabby didn't want to take her eyes off Gus, but she had to see what was outside the door. It was the floating white drone that had been searching the streets earlier. By all appearances, it had come in through the automatic front doors and now hovered about six feet off the ground in the station lobby. It was closest to Donovan and Audrey.

"Please state your name," it repeated.

"Audrey Hampton," the young girl stammered with fear.

Tabby wanted to tell her not to give any information to the strange machine, but she couldn't decide where to focus her attention. Would the drone harm Audrey in the front, or would Gus attack Peter at the back?

"Please confirm social security number," the white floating machine asked.

"Why?" Tabby replied, finally having enough.

It hung there for a few seconds as if thinking about whether to respond.

"This area has been designated as inhospitable due to an industrial accident. Social security ident requested to ensure proper dispatch of emergency services extraction vehicle. Please confirm social security number to ensure speedy recovery."

Tabby wanted to believe it. Her entire mission was to get the three kids to safety and having a police car show up was her greatest wish, but this wasn't what she expected.

"Where are the police?" she inquired of the drone. "We need help right this second!"

The drone's fans tilted a tiny bit, which made it drift closer to Donovan. "Please state your name."

Behind her, Vinny pleaded with Gus. "Give me the gun. We can't fight them by threatening Tabby and these kids."

The older guy grunted. "Stay away."

Tabby imagined the entire room was rigged to detonate with explosives. It was a mineral-extraction procedure she'd often explained to visitors while doing tours in the Bonne Terre lead mine. Thinking about home made her nostalgic to get back there someday, and that would never happen if Gus kept threatening her people.

She re-oriented on the man. "Please, this is what we want, isn't it? Help is on the way."

Given a choice between the authorities and a crazy guy with a gun aimed her way, she was going with the authorities.

"They're not here to help," Gus began. "It's with those people down by the Arch. You saw all the drones, didn't you? This is one of them."

Tabby wasn't sure what to believe anymore. Did the sewer men really see their friends get shot, or was it all a ruse to get her and the kids away from help, so the men could rob them? That suddenly made a lot of sense.

She turned back to the drone. "Whoever you are, we need help. This man is threatening my friends." By taking a step back, she made sure the drone saw Gus.

That seemed to anger him. "You don't know what you're doing. They're going to kill us all!" Gus lifted his shotgun and re-aimed it at Peter, who had his hands up. "Give me all your guns, dammit!"

Tabby sought some spark of sanity in Vinny's blue eyes. Why wasn't he stopping his partner from going down this path? Was he too scared to act, or did he want to disarm them, too?

Like any good Mexican standoff, she raised her pistol again and made sure it was on the target. Her hands had never stopped their shaking, but she fought to hold them steady for at least one solid shot.

The fuse had been lit, and the explosion was coming. There was no way in hell she was going to let Peter die like this.

TWENTY

Poor Sisters Convent, Oakville, MO

"Please return to your assigned housing unit. Help is on the way." The woman's computerized voice sounded as even and unemotional as before, but the order had a little intimidation to it. She'd spent the past few years inside the cloistered convent taking orders from Abbess Mary Francis. She never once had an uneasy feeling about a request.

Perhaps it was the dog. She glanced over to Deogee. She refused to get out of the van, even though she'd opened the door for her to climb down.

"Maybe we'll just wait out here. I don't have anything I really need inside."

The machine seemed to think about it. The floating box didn't do anything different, but it was a sense she got. It was a little like how she guessed her new dog's mood based on its behavior. For a machine sent to rescue her, its standoffish attitude was disconcerting rather than reassuring.

"Negative. Help has been assigned to your postal address. You must return there to ensure proper help from approaching assistance." The drone moved from its position next to the driveway and floated over the walkway. By all appearances, it wanted to lead her up the walkway and inside.

Deogee still sat on her haunches inside the minivan. It was as if she wanted her to refuse the order of the computer voice; she showed her how it was done.

"I'm sorry, but me and my dog are going to wait inside the van for the next seven minutes." She walked around Mary Francis's vehicle, then climbed back inside. The voice had told her help was coming in a few minutes, so there couldn't be any reason why she had to be inside the building to receive them.

That made the drone speed over to her. "Warning. You are ordered to return to your structure. This is a mandate by the St. Louis County Police Department for your own protection."

It seemed wrong to disobey this authority figure, but if Deogee was going to act strange about it, she was going to do the same. The instructions made no sense to her, and when the authorities finally arrived, she was going to have a word with them about the way these computer-boxes talked to her.

"You have three minutes to comply with directive. Unable to deviate."

She remained concerned, but also found a little humor in the soulless voice. "What does that mean? Why does it matter if we sit in this minivan or go in there? Are we in danger?"

The box readjusted outside her window. "Affirmative. There are renewed threats of poison gas. You must get inside the structure to avoid further contamination."

"Oh, dear," she replied, testing a long-buried sense of sarcasm.

She sat there thinking for a few seconds, but quickly made up her mind about what had to be done. If the machine claimed to know about poison gas, she wasn't going to argue with it.

Rose grabbed Deogee's leash and put it back on the dog. She also whispered in her ear. "Trust me, pup. I'm going to get you to safety."

She licked Rose's cheek in return.

Rose hesitated, recognizing the bond she'd made with the dog. "I love you, too."

She opened her door, which made the drone move aside. It warmed her heart when Deogee rose to follow, and they walked around the white box like it was barely worthy of their notice.

"Two-minute warning. Help will arrive presently. Please return to central structure for rescue."

"I will," she said in a pleasant voice.

Rose led Deogee onto the walkway, which caused the dog to strain against the leash. As she expected, she didn't want to go inside the convent again. Outside, there were no sirens or flashing lights approaching on the street. It was

274

completely silent, save for the purr of fans from the machine ...

When she neared the entrance, the laser-pointer beam of light was clear and bright as it struck the wooden front door. She paused to study it. The dog acted like the light was going to burn her.

"It's bad, isn't it?" she whispered. "That's why you don't want to touch it." Behind her, the floating machine remained at the van, but the red light came out of its shell. To her eyes, it was as if the robot was pointing an angry, red finger at where it wanted her to go for punishment.

Her heart rate went supernova as she realized she was going to willingly break another rule.

"Lord, help me run." She let go of the leash and jogged along the front of the convent, off the pathway and away from the door. "Run, dog!"

Sister Rose hoped she wasn't being silly, but all the pieces added up. Deogee's reluctance to return to the convent. The machine's odd insistence on going inside. The strange red light. A countdown. And the computer said it was poison gas. That was an outright lie. Gas didn't steal away her fellow sisters; God had come for them.

Deogee ran ahead but wouldn't get too far in front of her. Her lungs burned from the short run, but they made it to the far end of the vineyard, at the edge of the tree line. The parable of Lot's Wife came to mind as she reached the safety of the woods.

"Do I look back?" she thought.

She had to know if she'd been paranoid, so she glanced back to the convent. The white machine remained next to the SUV, which suggested maybe there was no threat, after all. However, as she stood next to a towering old oak tree, she noticed the red beam of light on particles of dust in the air. The pointer finger was on the tree, not two feet from her head.

"What the—"

Through the trees, an orange light caught her eye. A muted gray military airplane was high above.

Now she understood fully what was going on.

Panicked breath caught in her throat and she barely croaked out the words. "Run, dog!"

She and Deogee took off into the woods and made it a few paces, but the ground shook behind her, throwing her off balance. A white-hot light came from back at the oak tree, like a giant flash camera.

Time seemed to slow, giving her an opportunity to consider her next move. She could drop to the ground behind a nearby tree and perhaps save herself. But she remembered her conversation with young Tabby. At the time, Rose disagreed with her idea it was a simple thing to die for your children.

Now, she faced the same test. Was this God's plan all along? Did he want to see if she would live up to his standards? Is this how she could join her sisters in Heaven?

Her canine friend stood there confused at the turn of events. Maybe she wanted to make sure she got out of there; maybe the explosion made her freeze in fear.

No matter the cause, she was able to jump on top of Deogee as the fire arrived.

She would never know if she'd done the right thing.

New York City, NY

Ted and Emily kept close to the buildings as they walked the streets, ever mindful they might need to jump into an open shop or alleyway to hide. However, when they reached Times Square, he couldn't resist walking in the open. Fifty-foot tall advertising video screens hung from buildings all along the popular tourist attraction. They remained lit and working, as if they didn't get the message there were no people left to watch them.

"I've never seen it close to empty," Emily remarked.

Clothing blew in the wind, and the canyon-like cross streets seemed to force mounds of pants and shirts into small drifts, like dunes in the desert. Shoes and heavier items remained where they fell, however, giving a snapshot of how packed the central square was at the time of the attack.

They walked north, toward the most crowded portion of the open-air entertainment venue. Ads for perfume, smartphones, and movies flashed on the screens above them. The trees of Central Park, where she was taking him, beckoned from a few blocks away, leading him to glance over at Emily.

"I'm fine," she replied to his unasked question. "I could tell you were about to ask. My apartment isn't far, but I figured this place was worth a shot. For many New Yorkers, this is the heart of the city, and for some, this is the heart of our entire culture. If there were survivors anywhere in the Big Apple, they would have come here."

She pulled down her mask and smiled at him. "See? I'm fine. I really am. Now I know there's no going back. The city is ruined."

"I'm sorry," he replied. "I'm hoping to find survivors, too." The helicopter blades continued from elsewhere in the metropolis, but they never seemed to get closer. The noise could have hidden the sound of the Predator drones, though he'd been watching every side street for flying objects. So far, he'd seen none.

"Follow me." She raised her mask, then offered her hand, which he accepted.

They walked together for a few blocks before she stopped in front of an apartment building. "This is it," she breathed out.

The doors and elevators worked as usual, so it was an easy trip to get to her apartment. He expected her to let go of his hand the whole trip up, but she seemed to need his support. It wasn't until they reached the door of her apartment that she released him.

He was relieved, though it was difficult to pin the exact reason. Part of it might have been her seniority, which played against his ingrained respect for the chain of command. At the same time, as far as he knew, she was still married to the man inside this home, so it was wrong on that level, too.

"Let's get this over with," she exhaled before going in.

He followed at a respectful distance, mindful she might want to be alone.

The inside of the apartment reminded him of who she'd been before all this. Political photographs hung from the walls. Pictures of her in the White House. At rallies. There was even one of her with the crew of Air Force Two, though it was before he joined up.

She saw him looking at it. "We'll get another one taken with my new plane. You'll be the pilot. Bank on it."

It made him laugh, but also made him feel a little emotional at the implications. How great it would be for things to get back to normal. Back to a time when his biggest concern was whether another pilot would get the trots so he could take over. Today, the weight of the whole country seemed to balance on his shoulders. "That sounds good."

Emily strode into a large living area with couches and tables. It had wide windows facing out to Central Park and enough room for dozens of people to mingle. It instantly made him imagine politicians standing around at fancy cocktail parties as they rubbed elbows with wealthy donors. He went in but shivered at how much he'd hate living that lifestyle.

He gravitated toward the windows because they were twenty stories up and the view of the rectangular park was amazing. The greenery went on for a couple of miles, and it was boxed in on all sides by a wall of high-rises, including the one he was in. On the ground below, he observed a large open playing field on the left side of the park and a tree-filled region on the right. A giant statue of a horse and rider were far to the right, in the corner.

The smoky mess from the Newark fire smudged the horizon far to the northwest. There was no way to see the ground over there, but the fire didn't seem to be slowing at all.

When he turned around to comment on how impressive the view was, Emily was on the floor crying. He hurried over but stopped short when he realized what was in her hands. It took her a minute or two before she looked up at him.

"This was Roger, my husband. He was here, no doubt about it." She held up a gold wedding band. "I—" A sob rose up from her chest and seemed to catch her by surprise.

"Oh, ma'am, I'm so sorry for your loss." He crouched next to her.

Emily's eyes were filled with tears, but she didn't seem particularly sad. "This isn't what I expected," she admitted. "I haven't felt emotions for him for several years. Our jobs didn't really let us remain close, you know?"

He'd had a taste of that. Multiple deployments had killed his marriage, but that was a long time ago. It was difficult to remember those early years when he believed love could conquer all.

"I didn't mean for you to come here," he said. "I only wanted to get you somewhere safe in these buildings."

She reached out and touched him on the wrist. "I know, Ted. You're a good man, and not only because you saved my life. Don't hold this outburst of emotions against me. I'm glad we came here, because now I know his fate. It would have been a distraction if I'd avoided facing this apartment."

Ted smiled back, unsure what else he could say.

"There is one good thing." She slapped him gently on the wrist as if to illustrate the sad part was over. "I'm going to go change into my own clothes. These loaners were nice, but we're here, so I might as well take advantage of it."

He stood up after her. "Yeah, maybe we can stay here for a day or two, until things settle down outside. Or...this would be an excellent base of operations for keeping an eye on what's going on over in Newark. It's too bad we don't have a radio."

"That's your call," she said as she disappeared down a side hallway.

My call, he thought. Ted went to the window again to watch the empty city for any signs of life. The sky rats flew all over the park and buildings, as they always did, but there were no rollerbladers, bikers or joggers making their way around the bike paths below him.

His mind drifted during his watch, though at some point Emily came out of her room wearing a new pair of jeans, hiking boots, and a button-down khaki shirt, like she was going on safari. She'd transferred the American flag pin again; it was tagged onto the pocket of her shirt.

"What do you think?" she said with a bit of a curtsy.

"I think you look...ready for anything." He might have said pretty or beautiful if she'd been anyone else.

Oddly, she seemed disappointed in his response. They both stood there for a few seconds of awkward silence, but her demeanor changed when she pointed behind him.

"A helicopter!"

Amarillo, TX

"I said don't shoot!" Brent screamed again. The six orange-clad prisoners who'd come in with him stood at various locations inside the trailer, each with their big shotguns trained on Curtis's boys. Unless there were more guys in the back rooms of the trailer, he thought it might have been about even in terms of good guys vs. bad.

He held his breath, willing everyone to relax, including himself. He was unarmed, so making peace was about all he could do. Trish crawled over to him, while everyone else was focused on the guns. Many of the guys slowly re-aligned inside the trailer, so Brent's people stood near the front door, while Curtis's group stood near the kitchen.

Curtis didn't back down, even with a pistol up against his temple. "This is how it's gonna be? Working for him now?"

Paul seemed more nervous than the other guy. "We're on no one's side, but he knows what he's doing. He was fair to us when we was prisoners, and he was fair to us when we got out. At least he never pointed guns in our faces."

That upset the men behind Curtis.

The young leader gravely shook his head. "It doesn't matter. My mom and dad are in Phoenix. I can't check on them even if I wanted to. Unless I find out they're already dead, I can't break my blood oath to the cartel. They'll kill them."

Brent tried to think of a way to further defuse the situation. "We'll drive down there. Me and you. I'll prove to you..." He realized it wouldn't sound good to want to prove they were dead. "I'll let you prove to me that they're still alive. From

there, we'll both have our answer abou.
going to happen next."

Phoenix was ten hours away by car, but he'd happily take the man to his house if it would save some lives. Cars were free for the taking, including sports cars, so they could probably make it in half the time it would have in the old days.

Curtis seemed to think it over, but his guys continued to retreat into the kitchen.

"It sounds like a trap," the man replied, acting a little like he wanted to be convinced. It was progress, Brent reasoned.

Paul pulled back a few inches, so the gun wasn't pressed up against Curtis's skin.

Yes, that's definitely progress.

One of the guys in the kitchen tipped over a broom that had been stood up against the counter. Brent saw it travel the whole way down and heard the metal pole slap against the linoleum with a loud bang.

Paul visibly jumped and squeezed the trigger of his pistol.

Curtis's head snapped sideways.

Then everyone started shooting.

TWENTY-ONE

New York City, NY

Ted and Emily leaned against the window like two kids watching fish at the aquarium. The helicopter banked left at the far end of the park, but then flew toward the near end. He immediately thought it was looking for someone.

"It's a Sikorsky Seahawk. It's the kind of rotor aircraft you find on a carrier." The JFK was on the East Coast, he was sure of that, but it was unlikely to be parked off New York.

"Who are they looking for?" she asked. "Do you think there are others, like us, running from the terrorists who attacked our nation?" There were still no people down in the park, so nothing felt right to him. However, when the Seahawk came toward them and swept through a turn right outside the windows, they both crouched below a chair so they wouldn't be seen.

He got a good look at it. "That's an unarmed version. It must be recon or search and rescue."

"That probably means it didn't come from a carrier, right? Why would they have anything unarmed on a warship?"

"I don't know, but there's only a pilot. No co-pilot or crewmen in the back. Why would he be flying around alone?"

She stuck her head up as the helicopter flew toward the opposite end of the park. "He's definitely looking for someone."

It couldn't be searching for him and Emily; they'd never made contact with friendlies. He'd been careful about staying off the enemy radar, and he was more and more comfortable they'd evaded the Predators, and thus, the bad guys. But if this was friendly search and rescue, they might not get a better chance to escape.

"I believe this might be a legitimate US Navy craft."

She studied him for a time, but then seemed to defer to his expertise. "Well, how the hell are we going to contact them?"

He laughed. "I don't suppose you keep a flare gun in the suite, do you?"

Emily rolled her eyes.

"A fire extinguisher?" he pressed.

"Yes, but—"

"I'll take it. Grab it for me. We're going to the roof."

If he had unlimited time, he would have taken a trash can filled with flammables up to the roof. The smoke would give away their position and the helicopter would see them. Since there was no time to spare, he had to go with the next best thing.

Emily's apartment was already at the top floor, so the run up top only took a minute. They popped out onto the roof while the helicopter was on the far end of the park.

"Let's hope it comes back," he said dryly.

"Are you going to shoot that in the air? You think they'll see us?"

And what if they did see them? Would it be safe to get on board an unarmed helicopter in the middle of a city surrounded by wandering bad guys? Predator drone Hellfire missiles were designed for air-to-ground combat, but there were other planes at the airport. Certainly, any competent invasion force would be able to shoot down a lone helicopter.

The more he thought through the permutations of rescue, the less convinced he became it was the right way to go. However, rather than bounce ideas back and forth to no end, he decided to present options to his commander-in-chief.

"Ma'am, if we do flag them down, I'm worried they won't be able to defend you. I have no idea why an unarmed helicopter is flying around the city, but we can't forget about the drones and men on the ground still searching for us. He might be trapped here, like we are."

"You're suggesting we keep ourselves hidden," she said matter-of-factly.

"It's an option... Though I'll be honest with you, your safety is in jeopardy either way." He tugged at the rifle sling on his shoulder, as if to remind them both they were still armed, but once in the air, their little weapons would be nearly useless.

The Seahawk helicopter made its turnaround at the far end of the park and the whump-whump bark of the rotors got closer again.

Emily sighed. "It's a risk, but if this is with the carrier, or any of our ships out in the Atlantic, it might be the lead scout coming back to America. We have to signal them that we're here, even if we decide not to board."

"Talk to them?" he said with surprise.

She nodded, still watching the helicopter getting closer. "If we climb aboard and don't like it, we still have our rifles to order them to let us back out."

"I can board first to check it out. Yeah, that might work." Ted ran to the front edge of the high-rise building. The helicopter approached along the left border of the park and was about to turn around.

He pulled the pin from the fire extinguisher and gripped the handle. She came up next to him and together they watched the Seahawk approach. It was two hundred feet in the air, about the same altitude as them. He figured they couldn't have asked for a more perfect signal scenario.

"Now!" he said to himself. He aimed down so it would stand out against the windows below him. As the helo passed within a couple of hundred feet, he unloaded the whole five pounds in one long blast. The smoke-like retardant billowed into a large white cloud below them.

They waited for a few seconds as the pilot finished his turn and started for the far side again. At first, it looked like they'd been missed, but the aircraft turned left again, cutting its loop short.

"That did it," Ted breathed out with relief. "I'm gonna—" He cut himself off when he saw another airframe in the distance. A Predator had come into the city and was now at the far end of Central Park. The helicopter might have been staying low inside the confinement of the urban nature preserve, but it wasn't invisible. Someone had found his hiding spot. "A Predator is coming."

He pulled her back from the edge, tossing the spent canister on the ground.

"You said those weren't built for air-to-air, right?"

"That might be true, but we just gave ourselves away." Adrenaline dumped into his bloodstream as the pieces of the battlefield lined up. The helicopter was only a distraction now, it could never get to them in time, though it was still on the way. The drone was the big threat to them. "Run!"

By the time they'd made it to the stairwell door, the Seahawk driver maneuvered his aircraft to about twenty feet above the edge of the building. Ted had a clear view of the man even as he waved him off.

Over the park, the Predator let its last Hellfire missile go. The puff of smoke and orange flare of exhaust signaled their fate.

He pushed Emily into the stairwell, with only enough time left to observe how she'd forgotten to put her mask back on.

St. Louis, MO

Vinny surprised everyone by attacking Gus, throwing his arms around him, bear-hug style. Unfortunately, that shook the old man and he pulled the trigger of his shotgun.

Tabby experienced a warm gush of air as it went by, then she recoiled at the incredibly loud boom.

"Oh, God!" she shrieked.

"Holy shit!" Peter screamed at the same time.

"Run!" Vinny yelled.

She gathered her wits and considered shooting Gus in self-defense, but he was tangled up with his partner. Tabby hoped the younger man got the better of the situation, but she couldn't afford to stick around to see how it went.

"Get out!" Vinny ordered.

Tabby stuffed the gun behind her back, then grabbed at Peter to get him moving. The acrid fumes had already filled the lobby, adding to the immediacy of how close they'd come to getting killed. Not surprisingly, the thick-boned boy appeared frozen by his brush with death, so she had to yank his shirt.

"Peter, go!"

She followed him out the door to the lobby but found Audrey and Donovan stuck in molasses too. Gus's shot went between them all and accidentally hit the hovering white machine. Now it was junk on the tiled floor, but the two kids couldn't take their eyes from it.

"Go!" She ushered them across the lobby and made it most of the way to the front door before she saw a new threat. Tabby had to grab Audrey by the collar to get her to stop. "Change of plans!"

Peter ran into her backside, then bounced off like a lost boy. "What's happening?"

She didn't expect to see a larger mechanical beast walking down the street outside. It was one of the horse-like robots from the lines of them down under the Arch. It ambled on hinged legs exactly like a big cat, a dog, or horse might do, and it was right outside the door. "This way!" she barked.

The kids didn't move, so she had to pull each one until they did so.

Tabby led them down the hallway to where the elevators were located, but she didn't stop to use them. The EXIT sign beckoned her into the stairwell, so she slammed into the crossbar to open it, then waited.

"Run!" She held the door until all three kids had made it through.

From her vantage point, she saw the small horse use the automatic door and come into the lobby. The four feet clopped on the tiled floor, creating an almost alien contrast—the strange animal didn't belong indoors. Its low-profile head seemed to remain focused straight ahead, where the smaller drone had been destroyed and where Gus and Vinny presumably still struggled over the shotgun.

A long hatch opened along the horse's back. From inside, a thick black tube rose up on a wire frame until it projected several inches above the head.

She shut the door most of the way but couldn't take her eyes off the intruder.

Get out of there, guys, she thought.

"Tabby, let's go!" Audrey whispered from the stairwell. "The exit is right here."

The four-legged beast braced itself by planting its feet on the floor. The tube started spinning with a howl, then bangs exploded from the horse's rotating gun.

"No!" She fell back through the door and landed on her butt.

The machine gun let out a constant stream of bullets, and the concussion rattled the heavy metallic door between her and the robotic horse. She had to imagine what those many shots were doing to the studio and the two men inside.

Tabby scooted across the landing and stumbled down the first few steps before getting proper footing. She imagined the horse crashing through the doorway to chase them. It was less than thirty feet away...

"Go!" she panted.

She and the kids practically fell out the emergency exit door into another alleyway. There were no robots in view, which was a plus, but she was turned around and had no idea where to go.

"Anywhere but here," she said to herself.

"What?" Peter yelled. When she glanced over to him, he had a finger in his ear as if he couldn't hear, either. Tabby had been close to the shotgun when it went off, but Peter was a few feet closer.

Donovan was in tears; she could have easily joined him. The military-grade gun still chattered inside the building. Two fire doors and a stairwell didn't block it all out.

"We have to run back to the car. Does anyone recognize anything?"

To her shock, Donavon pointed the way.

"You sure?" she said while holding his shoulder to try to offer a small crumb of sympathy.

He nodded and sniffled at the same time. "I remember those dumpsters."

They'd come out closer to their return path than she thought.

"Good job," she said.

Together, they ran for their lives.

TWENTY-TWO

New York City, NY

"I've never had running cramps like this before." Kyla leaned against the stone column, thankful Meechum had called for a five-minute pause. She wasn't going to admit it to the other woman, but her stomach was putting in a stern request to jettison breakfast.

They'd run from Battery Park, on the south end of Manhattan, and they'd stopped at Grand Central Station. As planned, they ran through the dense parts of the city, including the tall buildings of the financial district in Lower Manhattan, the apartment buildings of the East Village, and now they were back among the tall skyscrapers of Midtown.

"Welcome to the Marines," Meechum replied, chest heaving. "I gave you the shirt top because I knew you could handle it."

Kyla didn't feel that tough, despite having grown up in the rough outskirts of New York City. "Thanks. It isn't as glamorous as I'd hoped."

She reflected on how her mom still lived in that tough outskirt. A place called Pelham Bay. *She used to live there.* Kyla had no doubt Mom was dead, especially after seeing the last four miles of the city she loved. That fact didn't make her feel tough, at all. She was weakened by the realization.

"Come on, let's check this place out." The blonde Marine strode away from the entrance to look around inside, unconcerned with whether Kyla believed she was tough or not.

Grand Central Station was always busy. It was a tourist destination for those coming to New York City to see the sights, but it was also the daily transit point for tens of thousands of locals coming to Midtown to work.

"Do you see anyone?" Meechum asked a short time later as she trotted down the giant staircase. Her breathing was almost back to normal.

The lights were on like any other day, but the high vaulted ceiling and soccer-field-sized promenade underneath made the place seem like a morgue. Evidence of those travelers and tourists were still there, but only their clothing remained. Hundreds of pairs of shoes, every color of slacks and dresses, and numerous suitcases had fallen to the floor.

Other than the two of them, there was no one left alive in the entire place. They'd seen the same thing along their run.

"I can't believe this is real." Kyla had seen evidence of the attack back on the carrier, and knew the captain had trouble contacting anyone back on shore, but she didn't believe civilians had been killed until now. "And this is why my Uncle Ted called me. He knew it was this bad."

"Cool dude?" the Marine asked as she pulled a water out of her backpack.

"Yeah. He and my mom were close, but she was the space cadet and he was the Air Force

cadet. They couldn't have been more different."
She chuckled, thinking of any number of the
good times they'd all shared when he came to
visit.

She sucked in as much oxygen as possible,
then released it. Her breathing still refused to
level off.

"Do you know where he is now?" Meechum
asked.

Kyla thought about it. He said he was coming
for her, but that was yesterday, and her ship had
moved. It was unlikely he'd even be able to find
her. Plus, with strange aircraft flying around, and
the entire population of the city wiped out, she
figured he'd have more important things to do.

"He's probably in London. They'd have to get
the vice president to safety. I'm sure of it." She'd
left a short message when she tried to call him
this morning, but the lines hadn't been working
ever since. If they got back to the ship, she would
try him again. She'd have to tell him about
Mom...

Meechum gulped down a little water, then
handed it to her. "It isn't how it should be, but if

we lost President Tanager, it would be nice to have a female president, don't you think?"

"Do you believe the president is dead, too?" For some reason, she continued to think the attack was confined to the world she saw with her own eyes, though she knew that was unreasonable. If everyone in New York City was dead, it stood to reason all the people in Washington D.C. were gone, too.

"Wait—" Meechum said in answer.

The rumble of a helicopter rotor carried on the air, and they heard it resonate inside the giant echo chamber. It went away a few seconds later, perhaps because it flew around other buildings.

Meechum grabbed the water bottle from Kyla and stuffed it in her pack. "We've got to move out. It sounds like our ride is already at Central Park."

Kyla the chair-jockey programmer was almost in tears by the time they'd made it to the park ten minutes later. Her side was going to split open because of the pain. The water hadn't helped at all. But most of her suffering was the grief of knowing Mom was gone. She wanted to stop and cry several times, but that didn't fly in Meechum's Marine Corps extension program.

The combat Marine dragged her civilian butt beyond the Sherman statue at the southeast corner of the park, which gave them a broad view of the whole place. The Seahawk helicopter was there, but it behaved erratically over the near end of the park. She watched as it banked left, then made an evasive maneuver by dipping lower over the trees. Above, a fast-moving rocket came out of nowhere and slammed into the top of an apartment building.

"What the hell did we walk into?" Meechum deadpanned.

New York City, NY

Chunks of concrete, plaster, and rebar fell through the stairwell while Ted and Emily ran down flight after flight. The explosion did a lot of damage to the roof exit, but the Hellfire wasn't powerful enough to destroy the entire top level, which gave them enough room to run.

"We have to get out of here. I think they saw us without our masks." Ted wasn't mad at her for leaving her mask when she changed clothes, but he was angry at himself for dropping the ball on security again. The drone operator would have taken their picture as it targeted them for destruction.

And they probably watched us come in. He didn't tell her that, however, because it seemed obvious in retrospect. If Emily was an important enemy of the invaders, they'd naturally keep tabs on where she might show up. In the fog of war, maybe the bad guys didn't get the news Air Force Two had been brought down. He'd been thinking in terms of helping her get over the loss of her husband, but that compassion might now get her killed.

His leg muscles burned by the time he reached floor three, and if he kept running, they could be out on the road in sixty seconds, but he had to be smart about their departure. "Hold up."

"Holy cow," she blurted as she slammed up against the wall to celebrate stopping. "My legs are twitching." Almost forty flights of stairs had wrecked them both.

"We have to see what's outside before we go out there. I'm going to find a window if I can." He pulled open the fire door and went to the first apartment. After a brief knock, he tried the door handle.

"Locked. Try the next one. Hurry!" He didn't want to shoot the door handle, though that would be the fastest way in. If they were heard, the escape would be ruined.

They ran down the tiled hallway trying doors until he found one that was open. He waved her over, then they ran inside and went to the windows. Briefly, he scanned the living area: wooden floors, modern furniture, giant flat panel television. If he had to guess, it was owned by a well-to-do single man.

Ted pulled back the drapes only enough to see the streets thirty feet below. There was no action directly outside, but if he craned his neck to the left, he managed to see the edge of Central Park. It appeared as if several black panel vans were unloading men.

"Crap," he let slip.

"What is it?"

"Men. Lots of them. We've got to get down the stairs and out the door before they surround us."

To her credit, she didn't ask him to explain every detail. She ran over to the front door and waited for him to catch up.

"Are you ready for this, ma'am?" he asked, serious for a change.

She grinned. "Ted, if you call me ma'am again, I'm going to kill you myself."

She took off into the hallway.

He chuckled, but also double-checked his AR.

"Don't fail me, buddy," he whispered to the rifle.

San Francisco, CA

"Play dumb? I don't have to play dumb, Poppy, because I don't know anything. Like where we are right now."

Dwight followed the man to a warehouse with all its shipping doors open. It was designed to allow semi-trucks to back up and load cargo, but now it appeared as if a hundred people were having a party in there.

The man stopped him before going in. "So, you look like one of the guys whose container fell in the water. Is that right? We've had several people come in looking like they'd been beat up."

Dwight wanted ownership of that metal box. The guy apparently was going to help confirm it was his. "Sure, that sounds like what happened."

"Let's get you cleaned up. You can grab a uniform over there, then come to the food table and get your lunch. We're leaving soon, so you made it back just in time."

He heard the words and tried to act like he understood them, but he was still buzzed. "My wine bottle!" he blurted, suddenly remembering it wasn't in his hands.

The man turned around. "I think that tip-over affected your memories. We don't drink, remember?"

"Am I in Hell?" It would explain where all the people went. Normals would go up to the angels—guys like him wouldn't.

The man in the jumpsuit lost some of his smile. "Get dressed. Hurry, please."

Dwight was shoved into a large room with racks of the black uniforms, boots, and hats. His own clothing left a lot to be desired in terms of quality, so it didn't take a cattle prod to get him to strip them off and put on the new ones. When he finally got in front of one of the dressing mirrors, he thought he looked presentable.

"I could apply for a job," he said proudly.

Poppy pointed out how his ratty hair wouldn't do him any favors at the interview, but all he could do was run his fingers through it to try to improve his appearance. When he finally emerged from the room, Dwight was going to make a run for it, but the man waited for him.

"Ah, much better. I think you got off easy compared to some of the injured men and women in those lost containers."

Those words meant nothing to him, but he nodded anyway.

Poppy whispered in his ear.

"No, I can't give you one of the jumpsuits," he fumed at barely a whisper.

"What did you say?" the man asked.

"Nothing. I should be going, thanks for all your help."

"Very funny, uh ... What's your name? Mine's Jacob."

"I'm Poppy. No! What am I saying? My name is Dwight Inverness."

"Inverness? I don't recall anyone with that name on the manifest." Dwight withered as the man peered at him with the intensity of a police interrogation light. However, his smile soon returned. "But, to be honest, there are so many of us, how could I remember all the last names? Am I right?"

Dwight nervously laughed.

"Here, eat up. They were about to put the table away, but there are still a few morsels for latecomers. When you've downed a little, I'll take you to the departure point. The boss is going to give us a big speech before we get on the motorcycles."

"Motorcycles? Where are we going?"

"How could you forget your destination?"

Poppy whispered in his ear again about lying. He was pleased that she'd kept her voice low around other people. Especially, Jacob.

"Of course I remember it. Where are you going?"

"Folsom, California," he said proudly. "That's where most of this detachment is headed. It's the first burn point for us, plus there's going to be a big show, too."

"That's where I'm going," Dwight announced, much to his own surprise.

"Great!" Jacob slapped him on the back. Dwight steadied himself and ensured Poppy didn't fall off, then he turned his double-vision on the food table.

"I'll feel better once I've had a little grub."

"Go for it. I'll wait right here."

He listened as Poppy cawed in his ear.

"I know," he said to her as he lined up behind a few stragglers at the spread of food.

Poppy was on the same page as him, for once. He had to get out of there as fast as he could.

313

TWENTY-THREE

New York City, NY

Ted ran down the remaining flights of stairs two at a time. Emily lagged behind but he didn't mind. It gave him a few moments to visualize what would happen next. Hopefully, just more running, but, if necessary, he had his AR primed for action. When she arrived and saw him with his rifle pointed at the door, she did the same.

"Are we going to have to shoot our way out?" she asked with worry.

"I hope not. The men are in the front of the building. We're in the back. I'm trying to remember where the subway stops are. I know they're close to the park because I rode them with my sister and niece, but I can't remember where."

"Yep, it's not far," she assured him. "The 57ᵗʰ Street Station is one block over. Right through this door, then run like hell down 6ᵗʰ Avenue."

"Use whatever cover you can find," he suggested.

Emily nodded.

He looked over her rifle to ensure the safety was off and a round was already in the chamber. If they needed to shoot their way out, it was going to take both of them. However, he wanted to avoid the need by moving fast. "You catch your breath?"

"No," she said with a smirk, "but you are going anyway, aren't you?"

"Sorry. We've got a schedule to keep." He laughed it up to help bolster their spirits.

Ted pushed the door open as quietly as he was able, but the hinges squeaked in a way that made him think the whole city knew they were there. Immediately, the sounds of the Seahawk helicopter and Predator drones filled the air, but no men were around.

"Go!" he mouthed to her.

They ran a short distance on a cross street but stopped at the corner of 6th Avenue, which was a north-south street filled with stopped taxis, box trucks, and regular cars. He checked to see if any men had come around the bend up by the park, but it all seemed clear.

"Keep the cars between us and them," he advised. They both hopped off the curb and got into the street, but the crack of gunfire made him stop immediately. He fell behind a taxi. Emily came to a halt next to a nearby trash truck.

Windshield glass exploded on a small sedan between the two of them.

"They saw us," he said dryly. He was certain someone had the entire street rigged with surveillance. They'd been lucky to get out while they could. The black-clad men were at the front corner of the building, two blocks down, but they were moving closer.

"Go for broke! I'll cover you." Ted slapped the rifle on the back corner of the taxicab, then lined up a shot through the 24x scope. It was dialed-in for a hundred yards, and they were at about one-fifty, so he aimed for their heads, assuming he'd hit their chests. He picked a running man on the sidewalk, in full view of the whole street.

The gun cracked, causing him to shift, but when he re-oriented on the scope, the man was down. The others ducked, too, and the smart ones ran into the street to take cover among the cars.

The men weren't dressed like any US military outfit he'd ever seen, so he didn't worry he'd shot at someone on the blue team. These guys fired first at two people dressed like civilians. They were bad guys.

Free-fire time.

He picked a second man who had run around the corner, then pulled the trigger.

"Hell yeah," he shouted. The round hit the guy's shoulder, which sent him tumbling into the gutter.

More men emerged from around the corner, and he squeezed off a few extra shots to give them something to think about, but there wasn't enough time to properly aim. The guys in the street were threading through the cars, and he couldn't hold them all off.

Behind him, Emily's khaki shirt weaved left and right as she ran for it. A bullet ricocheted off a lamp post about ten feet away, keeping him focused on himself.

Ted stayed low, hoping they wouldn't see him reposition. He ran behind the trash truck and used it as a blocker to hide his retreat, then he sprinted to catch up to the woman he was sworn to protect.

"It's right here," she confirmed as soon as he got close.

"I'm behind you!" he said as he stopped to line up another attacker. However, he came up empty. There weren't any targets to shoot along the sidewalk because the enemy soldiers were all in the traffic. If he couldn't see them, maybe they couldn't see him back. He and Emily hustled into the stairwell for the subway station, then went into the depths.

He let her go down first but stayed on her heels. He didn't think anyone saw them go in, but he had to assume they would follow them eventually.

Emily ran to the edge of the platform, and Ted noticed her whole body shaking.

"It's going to be all right," he said to instill confidence.

"They're trying to kill us," she replied with dismay.

"We're going to kill them first. If you see anyone—anyone—you shoot right away, you understand?"

She drew in a breath. He heard the fear in her lungs. "I'm trying, Ted. I didn't expect to be a nervous wreck when the shooting started."

He laughed, guiding her off the platform. "You should have seen me back in Iraq. I was at ten-thousand feet when I avoided my first surface-to-air missile. Nearly peed my pants."

"I can only imagine."

They stood next to a tiled wall that had the same bathroom feel as the Lincoln tunnel. Ted pointed down the tunnel in both directions. "Which way will take us to Central Park? That way, right?"

"Yes, but don't we want to go the other way?"

"No. I made a mistake, Emily. They've been waiting for high value targets. Probably have a presence in lots of buildings around here. They'll all be coming down to help their friends. Our only chance is to do the unexpected."

She started off in the direction of the park. "Like going north when every logical reason says we would go south."

He ran to catch up. "Bingo bango bongo, ma'am." For a second, he expected her to complain about using that word, but she was occupied.

"Power's still on. Don't touch two of the three rails," she said ominously. "Or zap, you're dead."

"Great advice," he replied.

Ted glanced back to the stairwell at the end of the platform but didn't see the shadows of approaching men. If they ran like hell, they might get far enough into the tunnel that no one would see them. Although it was very dark, there was enough light to see movement far down the tube. He wouldn't assume they were safe until they reached the next station.

They'd gone about a hundred feet before he tripped over a bundle of wires hidden in the shadows.

"Ow," he spit out, thankful he didn't fall on the rails.

They were going to die if he kept making mistakes.

St. Louis, MO

Tabby and the kids made it to the car in the alleyway, but the sound of gunfire continued back at the TV station, in short bursts now. Either Gus and Vinny were still alive and fighting, or the robot horse kept blasting the place to bring it crumbling down.

"Get us out of here!" Audrey screamed.

"I want to go home," Donovan complained in his down-home accent. "Momma's gonna be mad."

"We're going," she replied. Her reliable car started right up, but she shut out all the commotion to quell her flaring panic. She lifted her hands from the wheel; they shook like it was ten degrees outside.

"Drive!" Peter demanded.

She intended to think of where to go next, but there wasn't much hope of figuring that out. There were probably those mechanical drones everywhere now because of the shooting at the station. Additionally, she didn't really know the city well enough to plan a route.

Tabby put it in reverse and sped down the alley until she reached the intersecting road. She'd followed Gus's MSD truck into the narrow alley from close to the Arch, so now she was going to return on part of that route.

Once the car was in gear and moving forward, the complaining got even worse.

"We can't go back!" Audrey screamed. She pointed at the Arch, which stood tall out the front windshield.

"I'm not," she replied. Tabby shoved the wheel to the right and the car sped around a corner and onto a two-lane street. A few wrecked cars blocked part of the route, but she made it around those without scraping them.

At the next intersection, she turned left.

"I'm going south. We saw a bridge over the river. We have to get to Illinois."

Donovan hugged his shotgun in the front seat, but he drifted back and forth because he didn't buckle in.

"Geeze," she said, reaching around him. "Peter, get his seatbelt."

She had to one-hand the wheel around another truck parked on the center stripe of the road, but then she glanced back to the otherwise reliable one of their group. Now he sulked as he watched out his window.

"Dammit! Peter!" she yelled.

He turned to her. "What?"

"His belt. I need his belt." She pointed to Donovan's seatbelt next to the boy's head.

Peter huffed in protest, but he reached forward and grabbed it, then stretched it so she could get a grip on it. With one hard pull, she got it extended enough she could safely strap in the boy. He was falling apart even as she watched.

"Thank you," she said with relief.

Peter went back to brooding.

"And don't worry about losing your gun. No one could have seen that coming."

Peter almost looked her way, but then redoubled his efforts to glare outside.

"I saw one!" Audrey's voice was hoarse.

"What was it?" she asked as they approached another intersection. "And where was it?"

Audrey tapped her window. "It was that way. A floaty one."

Tabby wasn't stopping for anything. All doubts about the motivation of those workers under the Arch went away when bullets chugged out of the machine gun. They had to get out of the city before they were caught.

"And another!" Audrey said in a panicked voice.

"Sheesh," Tabby growled. "Hold on again." She turned the car down a side street opposite of where Audrey saw the drones. Then, she saw a familiar blue sign.

"The interstate!" She drove as fast as she dared for a couple of blocks, then braked hard to make a left turn for the on-ramp to the highway. Once she had it pointed in the right direction, she punched the gas and went up the ramp.

The highway going east was on a raised deck, but the lanes going in the opposite direction were on a second level above them. Without trying, she'd found a way to hide from anyone who might be above them. However, after half a mile, the highway bent to the right, and came out from under its peer. The highway went into a complicated series of on and off ramps, but she kept going toward a wide bridge over the Mississippi River.

"They're going to see us," Peter lectured her.

As he'd noted, being on the bridge would put them in full view of everyone at the Arch, which was coming up on their left. As soon as they passed a huge round tower named Riverside Hotel, the silver monument came into full view, though she couldn't see the grassy turf at the base.

"I'm going to stay on this side." She drove into the right shoulder of the ten-lane bridge, which made it hard to see the bottom half of the Arch.

Peter became more animated. "You did it, Tabby. I don't see them. They can't see us."

"Keep your eyes peeled for those floating drones. They could send one up here to check if we went this way." She had no idea what she was going to do if a drone chased her. They seemed to act like hunting dogs, who called in the real killer once they'd found prey.

Tabby maintained a painful grip on the steering wheel until they got all the way across the river. The lanes going back to the city were fairly cramped with abandoned cars, but only a few were going her way, so she didn't have any problem maintaining this speed.

As the highway went through some old factories and dilapidated buildings, she unleashed the scream she'd been suppressing.

"We made it!"

TWENTY-FOUR

New York City, NY

Ted's eyes adjusted to the dim tunnel after a few minutes, but it got a little brighter when they arrived at an underground junction. The subway track they'd followed since the 57th Street station kept going straight, but another line passed over a metal truss about fifteen feet above.

"Do you know which one of these lines goes to Central Park?"

"The one we're on gets close, but, if I'm guessing correctly, this other one is pointed to the station at the edge of the park. I think that's where we should go."

He took her word for it. She lived within walking distance of the subway, so her guess had to be better than his.

Men shouted far behind, though they'd gone deep enough into the dark tunnel that they no longer saw the station. They at least had that going for them. He pointed her up a nearby ladder. "After you, Madam President."

She hopped up but hissed at him. "I order you to stop calling me that."

He grabbed the rung the second her foot left it. He didn't look up as he climbed. "I won't call you *that*, Madam President."

Ted snickered like a schoolboy. The stress made him lower his inhibitions just enough to make him goofy.

She reached the next level and climbed inside the cross tunnel.

"I see the station, Ted. We're almost there."

When he got most of the way up, he glanced at her standing above. She held out a hand to help him, which he accepted. "We stick together, funny guy," she said in a businesslike manner, as if she knew, despite his sense of humor, he might tell her to run ahead while he held off the pursuit.

"Yeah, sure. Let's get over there."

They ran through the dark tunnel for a hundred yards until emerging inside another subway station. It had the same large white tiles, but the long platform was bracketed with a dozen large movie posters, like they'd come out in a movie theater ticket booth.

"Yep, this is where I thought we were." She pointed to the subway platform number. "If we go up top, we'll be right at the edge of the trees. We should be able to sneak into the park without being seen. That's what you wanted, right?"

"The last place they'll look," he agreed.

They hopped over piles of clothes and went up a few flights of stairs. As promised, they came out in front of a wall of trees. Wrecked cars and lots of lost clothing filled the street along the edge of the parkland.

He also recognized the statue of the man on a horse he'd seen from up in her apartment. The metallic monument was out in the open, so he pointed toward the trees. "Over there. Hustle!"

Emily did her best to keep up. He'd been running her pretty hard since they dodged the Hellfire missile up on the roof. If they could get to a nice clump of bushes, he would risk a short break, but they'd barely made it beneath some trees when he saw a flash of movement.

"Down!" he dove behind a black metal fence lined with bushes. She collapsed next to him.

"There are already people here! They might be who the Seahawk was trying to find." The Navy helicopter was at least a mile away, on the north side of the park, which he found amazing given how crowded the skies had become with drones. The whirring of Predators came from at least two directions now. He and Emily were in danger of being spotted and killed if they stuck around. He had to keep the faith, once again, they weren't able to reliably see under the leafy canopy.

He craned his neck over the fence to look across one of the nearby fields. Picnic baskets and quilts dotted the quaint landscape where New Yorkers came to relax, though no locals were there. That stillness made it easier to see the two figures moving on the far side.

Ted raised his scoped rifle to see who they were.

"Marines," he remarked, "though one of them is wearing jeans, like a civilian."

"Maybe they're imposters," she replied. Emily sat with her back against the fence, re-adjusting the ammo pouch on her hip to keep it in place.

He spent thirty seconds trying to figure out what they were doing, but they were too far away to see any detail. However, they were small in frame and he soon figured out both were women. It didn't bother him, but it did seem highly unusual that two women Marines would be alone in the park like this.

"What are you doing?" he quietly asked the Marines.

The whomping of rotor blades alerted him to a new possibility. The pair was hiding in thick foliage exactly as he and Emily were doing. They kept looking back toward the building where the black vans were parked. And, perhaps most significantly, they were next to a large field where a helo might be able to touch down.

"That's our way out," he said with an ah-ha tone.

Amarillo, TX

In the first two seconds of the gunfight, Brent witnessed Curtis get a hole drilled in his skull, and he watched helplessly as the dead man's shotgun roared. It had been pointed slightly to Brent's right, so the slug went somewhere else. He didn't care, as long as it wasn't at him.

Brent then moved on instinct alone. He dove and pushed Trish under the little kitchen table as both sides of the dispute opened fire. Because they'd all been packed into the narrow trailer, there wasn't much they could do to find cover.

"Stop!" he yelled into the hailstorm of thunder and bullets.

Men screamed. Cursed. Crouched behind furniture or tried to retreat deeper into the trailer. A couple of Curtis's guys crumpled to the floor, though one of his men in the orange jumpsuits howled in the family room.

Trish held her ears and screamed. He understood why. She was young and at home. The sudden violence ripped her out of that fantasy faster than she could handle.

"You're fine!" he pleaded.

Brent caught sight of Paul, incredulous that he was still on his feet. He shouted to him. "Get down!"

The long-haired man appeared shell-shocked after accidentally shooting the other guy.

Paul slowly wheeled around, and his eyes flashed recognition at Brent's words, but a pair of holes opened up in his chest. He fell back at the force of being double-tapped.

Brent suffered a flashback to Vietnam as he watched the kitchen floor fill up with bodies and blood. It was something he never dreamed he'd see on home soil, and certainly not while he cowered under a table. Though he didn't have a weapon, the carnage spurred him to action.

First, he tipped over the table, angling the top toward the men who had tried to harm Trish. Then he grabbed her wrist to get her attention. "We have to move!"

She'd been beaten by the men; red bruises flared up on her cheeks. He understood, but she needed to get out of there or they'd both end up dead.

333

A chunk of table exploded next to his head. Because it was a round surface, their feet gave them away as still being behind it.

He looked at his men, hopeful one of them would lay down suppressive fire for him, but none of them were focused on him or Trish. They fired blindly into the kitchen, which only served as evidence he needed to risk an escape.

"Behind me!" he crawled toward the living room.

The bones in his knees rubbed together like daggers under the skin. He hadn't needed to move this fast since the 1990s, and two days ago he would have thought his days of haste were behind him.

Trish stuck with him, though he had no idea how she was able to see through her tears. The closer they got to his men, the more she cried out. Perhaps because the intense fire of the shotgun barrels was only a foot or two over their heads.

A man screamed in agony from the kitchen.

Another man fell against the oven. Pots and pans tumbled to the floor.

Someone shot out the fluorescent bulbs in the ceiling panels, and they exploded all over the kitchen floor. It seemed like an eternity while all this took place, but Brent and Trish made it behind the sofa after a short crawl of less than twenty feet.

His old heart paced along at maximum speed, causing his breathing to get difficult to control. He couldn't even speak.

Trish glanced up at him but said nothing, either.

The shotgun bursts continued for another ten or fifteen seconds, then they all stopped as if given a signal. None of Curtis's guys fired back.

"Brent!" a man's voice echoed from far away.

He peeked out from the side of the couch.

"Brent. Boss man! You made it." It was a man named Carter; a middle-aged bald white guy who was in for supposedly burning down his family business.

"We did?" He sat there for a minute gathering his wits. One more shotgun blast interrupted the calm, then...nothing.

He got up when his five remaining guys stood in the living room without fear of being shot in return. A couple went into the kitchen, but Carter helped him and Trish to their feet. "You're lucky, pops, we were ready for anything. You almost bought the farm."

He wondered if all the shooting had been necessary. Did the others even know it was started by a damned broom handle? Did it matter?

A man called out from the kitchen. "We got them all. Mission accomplished."

One of his people plopped down on the couch. "Thank God. That was some of the craziest stuff I've ever seen. We almost effing died!"

Other men joined him, and a small celebration broke out.

Brent looked into the kitchen only once to confirm the others were dead. Several of the escaped men had fallen to the floor there, though a couple of the others were cut down in the hallway.

Paul was the only allied fatality. Two of his other men had been grazed by shots but were otherwise fine.

Carter shuffled over and handed back his shotgun. "Here you go, Pops. Sorry we ever took it away from you. It seemed like it was the easiest way to get in. It was Paul's idea..."

"No, you did the right thing." He wasn't certain of the truth of his own statement, but he figured he would have been dead a lot sooner if he'd gone in with his attitude and a shotgun. Their attack on Trish had made him a bit crazy.

All the death tempered that haughty image.

"Let's get back home, boys. Get you patched up. And we're taking Trish back, too. From now on, she's under our protection. Got it?"

The five men nodded.

The trial by fire was over.

TWENTY-FIVE

New York City, NY

The Seahawk helicopter flew by, almost on its side as it swooped away from the impact of the missile strike. Kyla wiped away a sheet of sweat from her forehead and expected all hope of rescue was gone, but Meechum pulled out the handheld radio.

"Longbow, this is Pocahontas. We're close to the designated LZ. How copy? Over?"

The radio was static for a few seconds before the pilot came on. "I'm taking fire!"

Meechum appeared pissed and raised the radio to her mouth, but the pilot kept talking. "I'll stay here as long as I can, Pocahontas. Pop smoke when you see me coming over your position. Out."

The Marine spent time looking out at the trees and fields, and Kyla could only guess what the other woman was thinking. However, vehicle motors came from the streets nearby, though it was hard to say where they were.

"Move out," Meechum whispered. "That way."

She followed the Marine as best she could, but Kyla was ready to fall over dead. The miles-long jog through the city was all her desk-friendly body could stand. More running seemed like an insult to her heart, but she refused to complain to the tough Marine, knowing it would do no good.

"Just keep running," she mumbled to herself.

Meechum chuckled. "I loved *Finding Nemo*."

"You?" Kyla huffed. "You like kids' movies? I never would have guessed."

They crossed a walking path and came to a clump of trees before stopping.

"I'm a Marine, not a monster. Everyone loves *Finding Nemo*. It's a classic. What's more powerful than a father fighting to get his son back?"

Kyla wondered about her own situation. Was Uncle Ted really coming for her? She had to get back to the ship; it was the only place he would look.

They stayed in those bushes until the black vans pulled up in front of the building that had been attacked by the missile. Men got out who looked like they were dressed to be assassins. All-black outfits with black ball caps. They also had big black rifles, which were visible even from a hundred yards away.

"Who are those guys?" she asked Meechum.

"They might be mercenaries. Or a rogue department of the government. Hell, they could be TSA for all I know."

"Can we trust them? Maybe we could—"

Meechum shushed her. "No, none of this is right. Our mission is to get on that helo and get back to the JFK."

"But we didn't find any survivors," Kyla said sadly. If they'd found anyone alive, she might have risked going to look for her mom, but every civilian they'd come across since Battery Park had been disintegrated. She didn't want to see

Mom's clothes to prove anything. It was better to remember her as she was.

"Hang tight, dudette. Those guys are going into the building. I don't think they know we're even here. Besides—"

As she spoke, a gunfight broke out between the men at the vans and someone down a side street.

Meechum watched through the leaves. "What the hell? Who are they shooting at?"

Kyla stuck her head up, hoping to make sense of it, but there were too many wrecked cars in the street to see who was back there. However, a couple of the men in black fell like they'd been shot. That got the rest of the guys running for cover and aiming at the culprits.

"Come on, we have to get away from here, in case they sweep this way."

The distraction gave her a false sense of security as she followed the Marine deeper into the park. The whine of aircraft engines above suggested the bad guys were still up there, though the rotor whomps of their rescue

Seahawk were still out there, too. The battle wasn't over by a long shot.

It took them about ten minutes to wind through the tree-lined paths and well-manicured hedges toward a large field. Meechum kept them running along the edge, which was fine with Kyla. There were strollers, beach towels, and volleyball nets out there. They were the last things those people ever did in the field, and she wanted to stay far away from their memories.

Eventually, they came to a thicket of underbrush that Meechum found attractive. "We'll halt here. They can't see us from that direction, but we can see the landing zone." She pulled out the radio.

"Longbow, do we have time to find a better LZ? Over." After keying off the handset, Meechum turned to her. "I'd love to be far away from those men and that building."

"Negative. It's now or never. I'm making one more pass. Out."

"Damn," Meechum whispered. "Roger that," she said into the handset.

Kyla kept watch, though she wanted nothing more than to lay down in the green mass of leaves and take a nap. The gunfire had tapered off to nothing, though the planes still circled around, as if continuing the search.

"He's coming, right?" she asked when Meechum tucked the radio away.

"Last pass. He's at the far end of the park right now. We have to be ready when he comes back." She pulled out a cylinder from her backpack. "Smoke."

Kyla nodded.

The afternoon suddenly became almost pleasant, like a cloud had passed. A bumblebee flew in some clover nearby. A bird chirped in the trees above. If she blotted out the sounds of the planes, she could imagine walking out to one of those blankets and spending the whole afternoon in the sunshine. It wasn't unlike what she and Mom had done in the past...

A piece of tree bark snapped off a tree about ten feet away.

"Look sharp!" Meechum screamed. "They've found us."

The Marine brought her rifle to her shoulder, then she squeezed off three quick shots. She did it one more time before ducking back behind her tree trunk.

Kyla was unable to catch her breath. Part of it was from the run there, but now her fear stole all her remaining energy. More snaps of bullets tore up the mulch next to a walking path and bit into the shrubs all around her.

"He's on the way!" Meechum leaned from her spot and shot some more. "Got one!"

Kyla didn't want to put herself in danger but knew she couldn't squat in the shrubs while Meechum did all the work. "Come on, you can do this," she told herself. She raised her pistol and held it to her chest like it might get away.

Motion caught her eye in the trees to the right. A figure strode forward, his black rifle raised as if looking for targets.

There was no time to call for help or even to hide. The man seemed to point the gun at Meechum, who was in front of her.

Kyla raised the pistol and aimed along the sights exactly as Meechum showed her. She exhaled slowly and did her best not to move the whole gun, weapon, as she'd been trained.

The blast no longer scared the crap out of her. She flinched as it popped, but her aim was true. Though she couldn't see where the bullet went in, the man fell backward.

She was ready to brag she'd got one, but more were coming...

New York City, NY

Ted and Emily snuck through the trees toward the two Marines. The closer he got, the more he liked their chances of escaping the city. The two women were on the far side of Central Park, next to a huge field. He and Emily were on the near side of the field, which was more of a forest. If they could get around to the far side, the Seahawk could come in and extract him with the Marines, and the bad guys would never have a chance of catching them.

"Ted, I thought we were dead back there. I won't lie to you."

"Which time?" he mused. "This city was supposed to be empty, but boy was I wrong."

"They keep appearing wherever we go. Do you think that's a coincidence?"

"Maybe we need to go into flyover country. Indianapolis or Oklahoma City. They can't be there, too. Right now, I'll settle for reaching those two ladies and asking them for a lift."

The Seahawk's rotor buzz kept getting closer, suggesting there was no time to waste. He ran as fast as he dared along the edge of the field, but he was forced to stop when the Marine woman shot into the woods.

"Dammit, those guys in black are everywhere. They've already moved into the park!"

Emily stopped behind a patch of ivy hanging from a tree. "Can we help the two Marines?"

Ted scanned the scene through his scope. He and Emily didn't get all the men to chase them. Some had come down from the street where they'd parked their vans and had infiltrated the woods on the other side of the field. The fully-dressed Marine fired multiple times at some of the men creeping toward them, then side-armed a silver object into the field. Red smoke belched out a second later.

"Yes," he said dryly. "We can give them a chance."

The helicopter was close.

New York City, NY

Kyla squeezed off another shot into the woods, but the man she'd aimed at did not fall with a satisfying thunk. Instead, he hid behind the trunk of a tree.

"Crap!" she shouted in anger at missing him.

The man leaned out, ready to return fire, but his face exploded with blood, soaking the tree before he fell. She'd been prepared to fire her gun, so she shot it once on accident before retreating behind her own tree.

Meechum wasn't even looking in her direction, so she couldn't square the logic of who'd shot the encroaching man.

A second guy wasn't far behind the first. Someone shot out his knee, forcing him to scramble behind a larger tree trunk. Then he screamed in pain at the top of his lungs.

"We have help!" Kyla yelled toward Meechum.

The other woman had been busy; she'd tossed a red smoke grenade into the field. She crouched by her tree with her rifle draped over her legs, but she was on the radio. "Longbow, do you see us?"

The radio was loud enough for Kyla to hear. "Wait one!"

Meechum screamed. "We don't have any time. They're on our position!"

A bullet struck the end of Meechum's rifle, causing it to jerk back on her lap. Kyla didn't think the woman even noticed, or, if she did, she didn't care.

Another rifle crack caught her attention, this time from across the field. It came from the far side. A civilian man and woman hunkered near bushes over there. Much too far for her to hit with her pistol.

"Meech..." she said with fear.

Oddly, the man lowered his rifle and waved at her. He made finger guns and somehow, she figured out he was pointing behind her, where the guys had been shot.

It was the person shooting the attackers with her.

She waved back.

The man motioned to the sky over and over.

She shrugged.

Meechum was on the radio seemingly arguing with the pilot, so Kyla was left in a weird space all by herself. The injured man continued to scream behind her, but that way appeared clear for now.

"Pocahontas, keep your head down. I have a crap ton of firepower coming your way. You have to clear the hot zone. Over."

"Bombs?" Kyla wondered aloud. She looked over to the two people who'd saved her life. "Meechum, tell them not to hit that side." She pointed. "There are two survivors from the city, I think."

The Marine glanced over to where she indicated, but the red smoke was obscuring most of the field close by.

"Longbow, we're ready for exfil. Be advised, enemy is along south edge of park."

Kyla hoped that didn't include the two helpers, though the pair wasn't close to the southern boundary. She'd meant to clarify with Meechum, but the woman was already shooting again.

Then the helicopter practically dropped on top of them. It came down from behind the trees and brushed away all the smoke in seconds.

"Run!" Meechum screamed to her.

Kyla looked into the woods, worried someone would shoot her in the back, but no one was there. Meechum furiously waved for her to move, so she did as instructed.

The tough Marine unloaded on the woods as she backed up toward the copter landing site, like actors did in any number of action hero movies.

The wind almost blew Kyla backward as the Seahawk hit the ground with a bounce. The pilot appeared to struggle to get it back down, but it was low enough for her to crouch-run toward the flight deck.

The machinery was deafening. The rotors and helicopter engine screamed ahead of her, and Meechum continued to fire her rifle behind.

Kyla was so tired, she misjudged the height of the helicopter and slammed off the metal hull as she tried to jump in. It was those ten extra pounds coming back to bite her.

"Get in!" The Marine shoved her bodily into the compartment, then she hopped up after her, still carrying her rifle and hefting the backpack.

"Go!" she bellowed toward the pilot.

The tireless Marine hooked up Kyla's tether before doing her own.

Kyla knew enough to hold on, but she remembered the two people still down on the field. "We have to pick them up!" she yelled into the wind.

The pilot wouldn't hear a nuclear bomb; he wore the heavy headphones up in the cockpit.

"Headphones!" she reminded herself.

The helo banked out over the field, and for a moment, she had a clear look at the two people hiding in the brush. They weren't more than fifty feet away.

"No effing way!"

She recognized Uncle Ted easily enough, and that was shocking, but she didn't know what to make of the woman next to him. Was it the vice president? Kyla leaned far over the edge to watch the figures get smaller. Almost too late, she waved.

The man was crouched in the weeds and waved like crazy, as if he'd recognized her, too.

"We have to go back!" she cried out.

The helicopter rose straight up, giving her a sensation of being on an elevator. It wanted to glue her to the floor, but she fought against time and gravity to put on the headphones.

"Sir, you have to pick them up!" she said the second she had them on.

Meechum had hers on too. "Negative, our priority is to safely evac."

"They saved us! He's my uncle! They're the survivors! That's our mission!" Spittle came out of her mouth and covered the microphone. She yelled with great force, praying it would convince them.

"Negative," the Marine said impatiently. "Our mission was a bust."

The helicopter continued to rise straight up, and Kyla got the sense they were evacuating an impending disaster. They rose above the trees quickly enough, but soon rose higher than the twenty-story buildings ringing the edge of the park.

"But that's my uncle, I swear," she said with less enthusiasm. As before, telling military people how to do their jobs was a lost cause. They were already above the city and she couldn't get them to go back down.

The pilot interrupted her and Meechum. "We can't go back down, I'm sorry. They're here," he added dryly.

"Who's here?" she asked.

Kyla leaned left and right to see what he was talking about. She heard them before she saw them. Two dark gray blotch marks appeared in the sky; hovering over the park.

"Oh, crap."

TWENTY-SIX

Near Chicago, IL

Tabby glanced over at Donovan, asleep on the front seat. He'd curled up with his shotgun and hadn't opened his eyes since they'd left St. Louis. Peter and Audrey had been silent for most of the ride too, though she wasn't sure if they'd fallen asleep or were in shock after their brush with death.

For her part, Tabby was determined to drive north until she found someone, anyone, who was part of the disaster recovery effort. She imagined their stop in the convent with Sister Rose was a big mistake, because it had given Mom and Dad time to drive away with everyone else. Their delay in downtown St. Louis only made it worse. Now she might never catch up with them.

She glanced at herself in the rearview mirror. The grim woman staring back soon cracked a smile, however, since it was laughable to think of her parents driving north forever. Were they going to stop once they reached the North Pole? Tabby was ready to drive that far, if necessary, though she might need skis when they hit the snow.

The horizon ahead was filled with Chicago's skyscrapers. Numerous smoke plumes rose into the clouds in front of and behind them, giving the city a washed-out appearance. There had been random fires in St. Louis, and every small town between there and here, but nothing on this scale.

"Sheesh," she said to herself.

Mom and Dad had taken her on an exciting trip to the Windy City back when she was in grade school. Her memories of the vacation destination were mostly limited to what she saw in the digital photos they'd brought back, but she would never forget the trip up into the Sears Tower.

She followed the tourist signs deeper into the city, always avoiding the fires and traffic blockages, and she did her best to look away from the telltale shirts and pants blowing on the wind. A freak thunderstorm came along and collected streams of clothing in the gutters as she neared her destination.

A burst of thunder echoed among the skyscrapers, waking everyone up.

"We're almost there," she said matter-of-factly.

The wiper blades tossed water back and forth, but the rain was already slowing down by the time she neared the destination.

Peter squeezed his way between the two front seats to get a better look ahead. "Where are we going?"

"Right here." Tabby pulled the car onto the curb next to a giant black skyscraper, only stopping when it was a couple of feet from the revolving door. She shut off the motor, snatched her keys from the ignition, and walked out into the drizzle. This time, she took her shotgun, along with Audrey and Donovan's.

E.E. ISHERWOOD

The kids followed her through the large front door. Audrey slipped on the wet pavement, but Peter grabbed her before she fell.

"Thanks," the girl said with relief.

"Up we go," she deadpanned. Tabby was tired from being behind the wheel for five hours. The strain of looking around each bend with the surety of seeing the cordon of police vehicles also took a heavy toll on her mental faculties. Now, her emotions were spent and all she wanted to do was get somewhere she could see for miles. Short of flying, it was the quickest way to look ahead.

The lobby was huge and spacious, with gold trim, fancy furniture, and a third-story skylight. The mall-like enclosure sat next to the main building, rather than under it. The open top gave her a view up the side of the black-windowed structure.

Fifteen minutes later, they came out of the elevator on the observation deck.

"Wow!" Peter ran directly to the side windows. Audrey and Donovan followed with a bit more restraint.

Tabby took her time too, mostly to walk around dozens of tourist outfits strewn about on the black carpet. For a short time, Tabby walked toward the windows. The evening view was stunning despite the low clouds and light rain. However, her attention was soon focused on the dead people's clothing.

A man and woman had been sitting on a bench seat, probably looking out the windows, when they disappeared. The man's blue jeans and flannel shirt was exactly what Dad would have worn. The woman's style wasn't exactly like Mom's, but it was close, especially the tacky purse with a picture of a poodle on it.

She stepped around the bench like she was about to interrupt the couple's view. They'd been holding hands. The man's wedding band sat on the woman's slacks, and a tasteful gold bracelet sat with it.

Tabby lost herself in thoughts about her parents and what they had in common with the two lovebirds who were struck down on this bench. A small trickle of tears started at some point, but she was too tired to care.

"Are you all right, Tabby?" Audrey asked kindly. Peter and Donovan came up behind the girl, as if they'd noticed Tabby was in trouble.

"Yeah, we're sorry for running ahead," Peter added, sounding properly apologetic.

She wiped her nose with the back of her hand. "These two have opened my eyes to a truth I've been avoiding since yesterday. They've given voice to a nagging suspicion that wouldn't let me go, and I've refused to even see. It has followed me every mile since we left Bonne Terre and it has finally caught up to me. Right here." She pointed to the bench.

Audrey held her hand. "What is it?"

Tabby had been taught by optimists her whole life. Fall down? Get yourself back up. Bad grade on a test? Do better next time. Want the perfect career? Go out and learn how to do it. That optimism had carried her through and out the mine, away from Bonne Terre, across St. Louis, and for all the drive to Chicago.

Now it was gone.

The tour guide was never supposed to make the trip about themselves. She'd struggled to keep to that maxim, though the breaking point was upon her. Tabby's emotional state was already fragile, and it fell apart as more tears ran free. She let out a lone gut-wrenching sob, steeling herself as best she could to say the words.

"My parents are dead."

Then she exploded with a torrent of weeping.

Her friends piled on top of her to offer comfort, but for the next several minutes, the tears were unstoppable.

New York City, NY

Ted watched as Kyla went up in the Skyhawk. It was so impossible, he stood there dumbfounded until he remembered to wave like a madman at her.

"Kyla!" he shouted into the wind.

"Your niece?" Emily asked with surprise. "I thought you said—"

"That helo is from the JFK, no doubt about it. They must be looking for survivors, though how she got on board I'll never know."

Kyla saw him, of that he was certain. He assumed it was only a matter of time before she convinced the pilot to come back down and get them, so he was content to wait. However, men broke cover from the tree line across the empty field and took shots at the departing aircraft.

"Oh, hell no," he declared. Ted got on a knee and lined up his shot, but he hesitated when he heard the arrival of powerful jet engines.

He took his eyes off the men and looked to the north, deeper in the park. They were blocked a bit because of the trees between him and the planes, but he was almost certain they were two AV8-B Harriers.

A few seconds later, as the hovering jets inched closer and the screaming engines became eardrum-splitting loud, he was certain of their make.

"That's the sound of freedom!" he yelled.

The forest on the other side of the field exploded with extreme violence as the planes unleashed their rotary-cannon machine guns.

Huge branches fell from trees between the planes and the enemy ground troops, as if the

Harriers didn't have a totally clear shot on them. However, most of the shells went the distance and threw up grass and dirt under the bad guys.

A few men vaporized on impact. Others ran for a short distance or tried to hide behind the biggest trees they could find.

The Harrier pilots nudged their planes from side to side, which created a wide swath of destruction. They also tilted up, which ripped apart the vans parked on the street, along with many windows on the front of Emily's building.

He grabbed Emily by the elbow. "We have to run for it!"

"They'll shoot us!" she replied with fear.

The aircraft-mounted Gatling guns continued to wreak havoc, but he knew they didn't have unlimited rounds. If he and the VP had any hope of getting away, it had to be now.

"Trust me!" he insisted.

She followed reluctantly at first, but then with greater speed. When the planes finally stopped shooting, she ran as fast as he did.

"We're going east, that way." He pointed through the woods to what he hoped was an unoccupied street.

The Harrier II jets got even louder as they pushed off to gain altitude, and the engines only became tolerable as they switched from hover to cruise. He did his best to follow where they went, but it was impossible with all the tall buildings around.

Miraculously, some of the enemy still shot their guns. He hoped they were going for the planes, not him and Emily. None of the bullets smacked the trees or dirt around them as they ran, so he figured they were in the clear.

By the time they left the park and got back on pavement, he let go some of his tension. When they'd made it a couple of blocks farther into the city, he let Emily take a short break.

"That was incredible," she panted.

He'd been thinking about the timely arrival of those jets, and there was only one conclusion he could make. "The Harriers were ours, and I don't think they came from the JFK. Those are flown by Marines, not the Navy."

"They supported their own on the ground," she replied.

Ted still didn't know how Kyla fit into it, but she certainly had powerful friends.

He gave Emily an extra minute to catch her breath, but then got them moving again.

"Where are we going now?" she asked.

"East," he replied. "We've got to get off Manhattan before they figure out we're still alive. That will make it harder for them to find us."

He pointed where to go, then she took off jogging.

A text message buzzed on his phone before he could follow.

"Hold up!" he exclaimed. "I have to check this."

Air Above New York City, NY

Kyla was pissed they wouldn't go down and pick up Uncle Ted, but she understood a bit better when the two planes showed up and fired long strings of bullets into the woods where those bad men had been.

She reveled in the destruction, because each dead asshole was one less who could hurt her uncle.

Meechum and the pilot talked back and forth about routes out of the city, Predators in the air, and other air traffic, but Kyla yanked out her phone rather than concern herself with all that.

At first, she tried to take off the headphones and dial Uncle Ted's number, but she knew immediately it was far too loud to talk. She put her ear covering back on, then tried to text his number.

Uncle Ted. I saw you!

He replied a few seconds later. **I saw you, too. Why are you in city?**

Search for survivors. Search for Mom. No one found but you. Is Mom okay?

She held her breath, willing the answer to be a good one.

I'm afraid she's gone, sweetie. I'm so sorry.

Her heart was already broken from thinking the same thing herself, so the impact wasn't as painful as it might have been. She had to ask more important questions.

Who is that woman with you?

He took thirty seconds to reply, giving her time to dwell on his last line. When he did write back, all it said was, **OPSEC**.

She was positive it was the VP, but he couldn't say it on their connection. Who was listening?

Kyla looked out on the city now that they were high above and flying away. More of those hovering planes had attacked the Newark Airport, too. Smoke and fireballs rose across the waterway.

We brought help, she typed. **Where are you going? We can send copter back**.

Uncle Ted waited a long time, as if he had to think through each reply. **OPSEC**.

"Dammit!" she cried out to the wind.

"What is it?" Meechum said over the comms.

"Oh, nothing. I'm texting my uncle. He was down there. We could have picked him up if we'd known he was there. Plus, I think he had the vice president with him."

Meechum cursed to herself. Kyla couldn't understand the words.

She typed in the phone again, more mindful of who might be listening. Speaking without saying the wrong thing was a lot like programming a device to behave in a certain way. **I'm going back to the same place where you called me before. Bad there, but not hopeless. I'll get those people to look for you.**

Thank you. I'm glad you're OK. Your mom would be so proud of you. I am.

The Seahawk helicopter was already over the water. The city, and all the new pillars of smoke, fell behind her.

Goodbye for now, unk.

TWENTY-SEVEN

Queens, NY

"I never thought I'd say it," Emily wheezed, "but I can't run another step."

She and Ted had run out of Central Park and continued until they hit the East River. From there, they walked across the Queensboro Bridge, using the bottom deck to keep hidden from anything in the air. It was comforting to know allied planes were up there, but the enemies were still there as well.

"I'll keep it out of my report," Ted joked. "Though I should inform you I've been keeping track of your fitness since we left my apartment. If your health isn't up to it, I'm afraid I'll have to recommend the job of president to someone else."

She forced laughter out of her tired lungs.

The bottom deck of the bridge was four lanes, but it was split in half, so two lanes went east, and two went west. The two westbound lanes were bumper to bumper with what would have been the morning rush hour traffic in this part of the city. They walked in the emptier eastbound lanes.

"I should have ordered that helicopter to come and get us." Her tone was wistful, like she'd thought of the idea but knew it wouldn't have been right.

They'd talked about it when he had Kyla on the phone. It delayed some of his texts back to her as they debated how much information to share. Kyla asked about Emily's identity in her texts, but, at the time, they'd both agreed it wasn't safe to confirm it was her.

He'd responded with the word OPSEC, knowing Kyla would understand, but ever since the exchange, it bothered him they'd communicated at all, because he'd made another mistake.

"I should have lied and said I'd found a random survivor. By not answering, I gave an answer. To anyone listening, they'd want what I was hiding."

She walked for a short time as if absorbing all the words. During the pause, he second-guessed himself even more. "I shouldn't have responded to her at all. Now, they can use my niece to learn my identity. They'll know I didn't die back at Dulles. They might put two and two together and figure out the woman I'm with—the one I wouldn't identify to my niece—is probably you."

"You did the best you could, Ted. I know it bothers you when you don't get things perfect, but you should know by now, nothing gets done perfectly. We're fumbling through this at the same time. There's no manual. No one grading us. Not even your report can tell the real story." She air-quoted the word report, which made them both crack up with stress-fueled laughter.

"Well, we know more than we did this morning, that's for sure. I would love to text all that to Kyla so she could bump it up the chain of command. If there are allied forces defying orders and coming back to the mainland, they need to know how the enemy has spread out its forces. How they're taking over airports. How they're using the ports."

"And how they're killing anyone left alive. An activity I'm happy to say they've failed at several times today because of you." She took his hand as they walked. "And thank you for being there inside my apartment. I didn't know how much I needed to see him, and say good-bye, until I was up there."

That made him cast his eyes to the pavement. "I only wanted to keep you on familiar territory. I'm sorry for your loss, like I said."

"Cheer up," she replied. "I'm the one who's supposed to be sad, not you."

He laughed a bit, realizing she was right. Things were bad, but they were alive and on the move. It could be worse. The people in the nearby cars never had a chance to fight back. He did. Unlike millions of his countrymen, he'd seen a member of his family today.

"Didn't you say you have a house somewhere on Long Island?"

She looked forward. "Yes. My husband's family has a house in Montauk. We went there in summer to play golf and take tours of the Long Island Sound in their boat. It's a snobby area, but I think I can get you in as my plus-one." She squeezed his hand, then let go.

"Remind me never to vote for you," he joked.

"Ah, I'm hurt. Right now, you are the only voter in the city, too. I could have really used it." She smiled at him, then strode forward like she'd gotten some more energy.

"Well, I can be persuaded, I guess. I'd need to know more about your plans for the future. Are you going to raise my taxes?"

They came off the bridge to the sounds of drones, jets, and explosions.

They were all behind them.

Chicago, IL

Tabby cried her eyes out for several minutes. All three kids gathered around to support her as she kneeled next to the couple on the bench. They all cried too, but she figured out they'd been grieving the whole time they'd been together. She'd whipped them through their parents' houses to prove their parents were dead, even as she ignored the fate of her own.

"I've been a real jerk," she admitted when she finally calmed down enough to speak. "I should have been more sensitive when we were at your houses yesterday. I guess I overlooked all of it because it meant I had to take care of you. My biggest fear has been that I'd let one of you get hurt since your parents weren't around to take you back."

Peter sniffled and laughed. "We wanted it to be true, Tabby. If your parents were alive somehow, then maybe ours were, too. Maybe what we saw back in our houses weren't people after all, but just the clothes. Maybe the aliens took them to Canada or Mexico, and they're all safe and snug."

"That's not what happened." She forced herself to speak the words. "All of our parents died in this disaster, whatever caused it. It wiped out whole cities. Maybe the whole country."

After giving each of them a friendly smile, she turned around and sat up against the bench, so she had a view out the window. The rain clouds were still hanging around, and there were drops on the glass, but it wasn't raining anymore. Lake Michigan was far below, at the edge of the foggy visibility. "We have to decide what we're going to do next. We have no parents. No family. No authorities. We're totally on our own."

Donovan drawled his answer. "As long as we don't meet any of those drone people, or assholes like those sewer workers."

"Yeah, they were underground when it happened. Maybe there are other people who were underground and also survived the attack. People in other mines like the one we were in. Workers inside coal mines, maybe. Do oil drillers go underground?" Tabby wasn't sure who would be safe enough from whatever dropped out of the sky, but it was a place to start.

"I would be fine if we never met anyone else," Peter said, sounding a bit more upbeat. "I've got my girlfriend, a good friend, and one cool adult." He grinned at Tabby.

Audrey huffed. "That's not fair to Tabby. Do you think she wants to spend the rest of her life with Donovan?" She leaned over to see him. "No offense, Donny. You're a great guy, but she's, like, ten years older than you."

"Uh, more like five," she brushed back, before realizing it was a conversation she needed to nip in the bud, not engage. "We can't go hide. There are other survivors out there. Sister Rose was a nice woman. There must be others like her. We have a whole country to explore."

Peter snapped his fingers. "What if we wanted to run the place? Who could stop us? We could make ourselves the kings and queens of Chicago. Take over the whole city and run it how we wanted. The first thing we should do is empty the banks. We could create a literal pile of gold."

"Good use of the word literal," Tabby said with encouragement.

Donovan shook his head. "I'm not living in any city where you're the king. I'll rule another one, thank you."

Tabby got into it. "We could all have our own cities and do anything we wanted until we died of old age."

"Except meet people," Audrey complained. "I would hate to live alone for the rest of my life, even if I was in charge of things. We have to find someone else. Some other survivors, like Tabby said."

Tabby took a deep breath, not sure what to do but resolved at the need to take charge again. "I vote we spend the night up here. There has to be food in this building. We can sleep on these benches. When tomorrow comes, we can decide which direction to go."

She stood up and went to the glass. How many people should have been down there in the city? Millions, for sure. She watched to see if there was any evidence of moving vehicles on the road, or planes in the sky, or even boats on the giant lake.

Fires raged to the north, though they weren't much more than orange smudges twinkling through the drizzly haze all around them.

The city was empty.

But she wondered if Chicago would soon see the same horse robots and floating drones they'd narrowly escaped in St. Louis. If that was the case, then they weren't alone. The city wasn't empty. And their future had never been as uncertain.

A million worries clouded her vision, but exhaustion overpowered them all.

"All right. It's late. Let's sleep on it. I'm sure we'll have a new perspective in the morning."

TWENTY-EIGHT

USS John F. Kennedy

"Clear a path!" Meechum shouted.

Kyla felt important, though she had a hard time understanding why. When the helicopter landed on the deck of the carrier, the Marine said the captain needed to see her right away. Then she led Kyla up the ladder-wells until they made it to the bridge. Van Nuys was inside with a pair of binoculars aimed outside.

"Come in," he said without breaking contact with the field glasses. He watched what looked like another aircraft carrier about a mile away. She'd seen it too, while on the helicopter flight back. "That's the *USS Iwo Jima*. They disobeyed orders to be here, and I'm not sure if I want to give them a medal or send their captain to my brig. Their air assets pounded some militant targets in New Jersey and New York. They helped you too, as I understand it."

Kyla was confused about what it all meant, and she snuck a look at Meechum, but she was faced toward the captain at full attention.

"At ease, Marine," he said when he turned around. "I've heard good things about you two. Like how you got into the city despite being hounded by enemy Predators. Then you fought off terrorists until our helo could swoop you back up. That was damned fine work going into the city when you didn't have to, but I have to ask: were you trying to get yourselves killed?"

"No, sir," the combat Marine replied without hesitation. "You sent us out there to find survivors. I, uh, we wanted to give those people a chance to come out for a rescue. Unfortunately, we didn't see anyone left alive, so it was all for nothing. Well, except for at the very end. We did find two people..."

The captain strode closer. "I'm listening."

Meechum gestured to Kyla. "My partner can tell you that part."

Van Nuys turned his attention to her. She heard Uncle Ted warning her about operational security, but that was for people other than the captain of her ship. He needed to know everything.

"Sir, I'm pretty sure I saw Vice President Williams while we were in New York City. She was with my uncle, Ted MacInnis. They were in Central Park the same time the two of us were waiting for the helicopter, but we didn't know it until we were already in the air."

"And you couldn't go back for them?" he asked, looking at Meechum.

The Marine spoke up. "The arrival of the Harriers made it dangerous to return to the ground. Just as we departed, the support planes ripped the bad guys some new ones, sir."

Van Nuys tapped the binoculars and seemed to think about what he'd been told. Behind him, far out over the water, jet planes took off and landed like helicopters on the other ship. They were the same deadly aircraft she'd seen at the park.

Finally, he appeared to arrive at a conclusion. "This leaves us in a tight spot, ladies. The captain of the *Iwo* said there were no survivors in the entire presidential chain of command. General Worthington is the ranking member of the armed forces. He claims to be in charge of the remaining overseas forces of the United States military and he wants us out of here."

"We can't leave them behind!" Kyla insisted.

Van Nuys went on without any acknowledgement of her outburst. "Are you positive you saw the vice president? Maybe your dad was with a woman who looked like her?"

Kyla stood firm. "My uncle was the backup pilot on Air Force Two. I might not have recognized her in any other context, but if my uncle was still alive and fighting, I'm sure he wouldn't abandon someone as important as her."

The captain set the binoculars aside. "Lance Corporal Meechum, can you confirm what she saw?"

"No, sir. I was communicating with the pilot to ensure we got out of there. However, after spending the better part of the day with Ms.

Justice, I believe what she says. She's a straight shooter, sir."

"That's what I like to hear for my crew. I'll have to think about what we need to do to find them. We struck a blow against whatever force has taken over the city, but it was all from the *Iwo Jima*. My boat is still floating blind and without defenses. That's got to be my priority now."

Kyla replied, "Sir, won't there be other ships coming to the rescue? We have to keep hitting them. Whoever they are."

Van Nuys sighed. "The *Iwo's* captain gave me some more bad news. General Worthington has ordered every overseas American unit to stay where it is. He doesn't want to risk losing more people by sending them to the mainland, where they might be subject to a second attack."

"Sounds smart," she thought, until remembering it could doom her uncle.

"Unfortunately, it means we're on our own for a little while longer. The *Iwo Jima* disobeyed the order and came anyway—that's why I said I might have to send their captain to the brig." He paused. "Which I'm not going to do, by the way.

But two ships running at less than half strength aren't able to project much power. I sent the Seahawk out on reconnaissance today, and now I know what I needed to know. America is being taken over."

Kyla suspected as much.

"You don't seem surprised," the captain remarked.

She shook her head. "My uncle called me when this first happened. At the outset, I thought it was aliens or something similarly out of this world, but someone was on your ship, trying to take it over. When I saw more of those bad guys out in New York City, I knew they had to be working together. There are strange people landing at the airport over in Newark. That's what started our whole diversion into New York City. Sir, I would never tell you how to do your job, but if the vice president is alive, it means she's now the president. You have to save her."

"And your uncle," he said dryly.

"If possible," she allowed.

He shared a look with Meechum, then fixed his eyes on her.

"I'll see what I can do."

San Francisco, CA

Dwight picked at the turkey sandwiches on the table and grabbed one of the bottled waters to be polite, but then he tried to walk over to the same door where he'd come inside the warehouse. Before he could get there, Jacob came out of nowhere.

"Dwight! I hope you found the food satisfactory?"

"We did," he replied. "I mean, I did." Poppy wasn't visible to anyone but him, so he didn't want to give her away.

"Well, it's almost time. The cycles are parked on the far side of the warehouse, but we're all waiting for the announcement. It should be any minute now."

"Great," he lied. "I'm going to step outside and water the lawn, if you catch my drift?"

"Eww, gross. No need for that, my friend. We have running water. I'm sure you're sick of using those buckets for the two-week ride over here, huh? Go, enjoy modern plumbing. It's all we're going to have from here on out."

Poppy screamed in his ear for him to leave, but he couldn't with Jacob watching him as he was. If he went into the bathroom, perhaps another opportunity would present itself.

Jacob walked with him for a short way, but then the other people in the building became excited. It reminded him of how normal people acted when they found out a San Francisco sports team did something incredible, like win the big game. Everyone, no matter what else they were doing, suddenly broke out in cheers. That usually was good for him, as they donated readily to his cause. When the teams lost, donations went way down.

"It's starting!" Jacob cried out with excitement. He looked at Dwight. "The bathroom is over there. Meet me by the radio when you get out. Hurry, though, because this is it! He's going to talk to us, finally!"

Dwight experienced a sense of being lost the second the man walked away. He was pleased as could be to have a new ensemble to wear around the city, and the free food was already appreciated, but these weirdos reminded him of cult members rather than normals. It made him wonder if they knew what was going on outside. Where did everyone go?

"Just my luck. The world of normal people disappears, and I'm left with the nutjobs."

Poppy reminded him of his own mental health issues.

"I'm not crazy like them," he reassured his bird.

He didn't go to the bathroom. Instead, he got as close to the small crowd as he dared, while doing his best to avoid Jacob. The radio played a popular song for half a minute, then everyone got pin-drop silent as it ended.

"Greetings, fellow human beings." A deep, calm, male voice resonated from the speakers inside the warehouse. "I was once known as Dr. Jayden Phillips—a college professor, Nobel-prize-winning physicist, multi-million selling self-help author, industrialist, and, my personal favorite, *Time* magazine's person of the year. You, my friends, know me as your leader and spiritual guide through this existence we call life, but today and ever forward I will be called David. The David of Biblical times—the young boy who slayed Goliath with his sling and stone. Our present-era Goliath was America—the country most responsible for Earth's current ecological disasters. My sling was modern science. My stone was the atom, and even smaller particles of creation. For you, I have wiped the decadent Americans from our world, so we may restore this land to its rightful place as the Garden of Eden."

He paused dramatically, and many of the people in the building seemed to lean forward to see what he would say next.

"I have done the heavy lifting. Now, you must carry the torch across this once-great land. Dip it into the fires of righteousness and set alight all that remains of the people who lived in this land. Then, once you have destroyed every first-world mansion, snuffed out every smoke-belching power plant, and felled every heaven-blocking office tower, this land will be yours to rebuild."

Dwight heard the words, but sensed the man was a bullshit artist. He lived on the streets and knew the type well. Hell, he was a bit of a shyster himself, though he only did it to make money, not drive people to genocide.

Strangely, no one else seemed to share his misgivings. They all hugged and cheered at hearing the words of their leader.

The man went on after another long pause. "To those Americans living in foreign lands, take heed of my words. I say to your hosts: You have one week to kick them out. Throw them to the curb. Be forever free of their imperialist shackles. If you do not, David will throw his next stone at your nation, just as he did to this one."

Poppy whispered in his ear.

"Yes, it looks that way," Dwight replied. "These people killed all our friends." As a vagrant living on the streets, he had few friends, but he did have some. The leader of Jacob's people had up and killed them.

"My fellow humans. America is now free for the taking. Make sure what rises from the ashes is nothing like what you burn to the ground, or it too shall be consumed by fire."

Dwight backpedaled toward the door.

The guy on the radio said Americans were gone. That answered his question about why everyone's clothes were still lying all over the streets. These bastards had killed them.

"Poppy, you can stay if you want. I'm outta here."

He slipped out the door and ran down an alley but was turned around after being inside the huge complex. Instead of returning to the street that would take him to the shoreline shipping container, he came around a corner into a busy parking lot. Dozens of motorcycles were lined up in long rows, with attendants wiping down seats and checking oil levels.

One of the helpers, a woman, waved Dwight over to her.

"You're the first one! We heard Mr. Phillips out here. So exciting." The young woman used a red rag to sweep a bike seat, then motioned for him to hop on. "This one is ready to go. I've got the flamethrower tuned like a champ. Just be sure to return to the mothership when you need to reload."

Poppy flew right above his head, screaming at him.

"This isn't aliens," he whispered to her.

The woman heard him. "I'm sorry? What did you say? Aliens?"

He tried to think on his feet, what wasn't something he was very good at. "I have a bet with my, hmm, friend, that the Americans think this all was done by aliens. Now we're going to take this—" He patted the apparatus lashed behind his seat. "—and they'll see you, I mean, we're just people."

"Mr. Phillips says it doesn't matter. There's no one left who can stop us, anyway. That's why he went on the radio. We did it, man! We've taken back all the stolen lands."

He laughed a bit too loud, like he was an evil genius similar to everyone else around him. "So, when you said mothership, you meant—"

"The fuel truck." She pointed to a semi-truck hauling a long cylinder trailer. "Each motorcycle team travels with one mothership. Your team leader has explained all this, right?" She leaned on one hip, daring him to say otherwise.

"Of course. I like to be thorough." Talk about a lie, he thought. He'd never been thorough about anything in his life. That's why he ended up on the street in the first place. He couldn't hold a job. Couldn't stay clean. Never took care of himself.

But he was familiar with motorcycles, thanks to some riding he did in high school two decades ago.

Dwight started the engine. "I'm going to take it around the block!"

The woman gave him an appraising look, then flashed a thumbs-up.

He almost dropped the beast before he got out of first gear, but he steadied himself and drove off the parking lot.

Where could he go to find help? Who would he warn that the fires were coming for what was left of the country? If the jackass on the radio was being honest, it wasn't just San Francisco. It was the whole country. Everyone was dead.

Somewhere above, Poppy chased him as he rode through the vacant downtown.

Amarillo, TX

Brent sat with Trish inside the guard booth. After the shootout, he and his five remaining men came back to the prison, but not after some things changed in their relationship.

First, they'd raided the trailers next to Trish's to find clothing that wasn't prison orange, as well as food and other valuables. Second, they were loaded down with every weapon they could find, including the handguns Curtis's people had found.

Brent had no chance of disarming them again, nor did he want to. The guys could have easily killed him and done whatever they wanted with Trish, but they'd stayed on his side of lawful civilization. He figured there was no use denying they were all equals. To reflect that, he made it clear they didn't have to follow him back to the prison complex, as long as they let him and Trish be on their way.

The men followed him back anyway, and quietly went into their cells without incident. He and Trish went into the guard booth to have a little privacy while he tended to her bruises.

"Thanks for coming to get me," she said for the tenth time. "Those guys were absolutely the last people in the world I expected to turn up my street. I was lucky the landline still worked so I could call you. And I was double-lucky you were able to rush to my assistance like I was a helpless woman in need."

"It was my fault it all happened. I can't tell you how happy I am you suffered nothing worse than a few bruises. I might have shot myself if I'd gotten you killed."

"Curtis turned out to be a real dick," she replied dryly.

He thought of Paul accidentally killing Curtis in the kitchen. It was such a senseless accident.

"Well, put all that out of your mind. Just sit in here for a few minutes. Here, I'll put on the radio.

The music on the last station is horrible, but at least it's something."

He clicked on the portable radio, expecting to hear the hip-hop station, but some guy was talking. "This might be news! Hey, fellas! Come on over and listen."

The men ran out of their cells.

Brent's smile rubbed off immediately. It wasn't news. It sounded more like an evil villain announcing his plans to the world. As the five ex-prisoners arrived, they soon frowned, too. They listened attentively for a while, until the man sounded like he was wrapping things up.

"My fellow humans. America is now free for the taking. Make sure what rises from the ashes is nothing like what you burn to the ground, or it too shall be consumed by fire."

The station cut into another song, leaving them all in a state of shock.

"What does it mean, Brent?" Trish finally asked.

He looked around the room, suddenly feeling a lot better about having five men armed to the teeth guarding the prison. This whole time, he'd been thinking they were alone in this part of Texas, and maybe an area a lot larger than that. If the guy on the radio was to be believed, all of America was an empty, burning shell, just like Amarillo.

"It means we know who wiped out everyone in America."

His long-dormant military senses kicked in.

"Kevin, I want you to spend the night up near the front doors. I'll show you how to lock and unlock them. One of you other guys should spend the night up on the roof. Everyone needs to have radios. If you don't have plenty of spare shotgun shells, go to the armory and resupply. Tomorrow, I'll take a team to the local Walmart and get all the guns and ammo we can carry."

"You think other prisoners will come back?" she asked.

It had been his main concern while driving back to the prison, but the man on the radio alerted him to the real threat. An attack had been made on his homeland, and the leader of that effort had just bragged about it to the world.

"Maybe, but they aren't who I'm worried about." He pointed to the radio, then looked out at the men. "Whoever this guy is, he thinks America is his. Now, I don't know about you all, but I didn't spend four years risking my biscuits in the rice paddies of Vietnam just so some techno-douchebag can come in and take over. He might never make it to Amarillo, US of A, but if he does, we're going to give him a bloody Texas welcome."

He stood up. "People, welcome to the rebel cause."

TWENTY-NINE

Queens, NY

Ted and Emily's day ended almost the same way it began: they tore into the food supply while inside a stranger's home. They'd also taken quick showers; a slice of normal for both of them. They'd reconvened in the tiny family room.

"Of all the places you could have chosen, you picked the one that smells like mothballs and Bengay. I think the owner was both a neat freak and extremely old." Emily patted next to her on the floral-pattern couch. It sat facing a wall with a flat-panel television. The set was on, but it only showed multicolored bars indicating a lost signal.

"Hey, don't knock the old-man crème. I need some myself. My legs are Jell-O right now." He'd made the decision to keep going on foot, at least until they were a few miles outside the main part of the city. They'd had to duck into cover numerous times as they crossed through Queens and headed east toward the less developed part of Long Island. Planes streaked back and forth across the sky, including those damned Predator search drones. He couldn't take a chance they'd be spotted in a car in the confusing maze of streets.

Once it got dark, the skies seemed to settle down. Now, in the fourth-floor apartment, he thought they'd avoided the worst of it and could get some rest.

He stayed on his feet a little longer, keeping watch out the rear sliding door. Outside, a large swath of blackness was between them and the city across the East River. Fires burned over there, but it was most intense in the area where he estimated Rebecca had lived.

"This is our last chance, you know."

"For what?" she asked.

"To go north on the roads. We could cross the Throgs Neck Bridge and slip over into

Connecticut. From there, we could go up the coast like we'd discussed." He was exhausted, and his voice was hoarse from shouting much of the day. However, Emily was his boss, and he needed to give her options for their escape.

"No. We can't. If you saw your niece, we need to get you to her."

"Emily," he said tiredly, "I can't base our whole mission on my desire to find her. The safe play is to get as far from the big cities as we can, then go north to Canada."

It was almost painful to lie to her, because he desperately wanted to find out where the helicopter went, especially after seeing Rebecca's neighborhood burn to ash. He'd made a promise to his sis he intended to keep, but, as a major in the United States Air Force, he constantly had to prioritize. It wasn't yet time to bail on his duty.

"You aren't basing it on that alone." She stood up and strode over to be next to him. "Ted, I can hear it in your voice. I see how you look at the city out this window. All you can think about is your niece."

"No, I—"

She shushed him. "As Commander-in-Chief of the Armed Forces, I order you to take me to Montauk, at the far end of Long Island. There, we will either find my husband's family yacht, or we'll steal another plane."

"There's an airfield?" he said with excitement.

"Yep. A couple, actually. One is where I've done some skydiving. They're small, but they should have what we need."

"So," he said with understanding, "we'll have options when we get out there."

She bumped him on the hip. "We can fly, take a boat, or hunker down. See? My orders make perfect sense."

"Yeah, I guess they do. Hmm, this should help your performance evaluation." He pretended to hold a pen and paper. "Needs work on physical fitness but has firm grip of planning ahead."

"What? No! I'm evaluating you. Not the other way around." She mimicked his notepad routine. "Flight skills, top notch. High marks for evasion from bad guys. Physical appearance, presentable. Refuses to admit he wants to find his niece. Black mark for that." She made an exaggerated check mark in the air, giggling the whole time.

His exhaustion conspired with the soft lights of the living room to make him see her not as his boss, or the President of the United States, but as a pretty companion. For a few seconds longer than he knew was appropriate, he locked eyes with her.

Ted's heart pumped as fast as it did during any of the escapes they'd survived today. He wanted to tell her how right she was about Kyla. About how he worried he was going to get Emily captured by making a mistake. And, if he was listening to his fast-pumping heart, he wanted to tell her that it wasn't only the romantic light making her glow.

She didn't break his gaze, and for a few seconds, he considered leaning in to kiss her. No matter what he ever thought of her politics, he could never deny the petite brunette was attractive. Plus, if you couldn't find love in the aftermath of World War III, where could you find it?

But before he could make good on his feelings, the television set came to life. She looked at him for a couple of extra seconds, but then she turned to the TV. A middle-aged man in a black jumpsuit sat behind a desk in the oval office of the White House.

Emily appeared stunned. "What the flock is he doing there?"

The Bad Place

Deogee found herself pinned underneath her new human. She wasn't anything like her last owner—she didn't run, throw the ball, or take her to the park with all the other dogs. That was why it shocked her when she became agitated and tried to run from the strange floaty thing. It surprised her even more when she fell on top and crushed her to the smelly grass.

"Ouch!" she complained.

A strange heat brushed her fur, though only for a bark or two. It stung the worst anywhere the human wasn't shielding her. It smelled strange, like a fire, but also like the mechanical juice left on roadways by cars. Before she could pin down the odor, the fire receded.

She squirmed out from underneath the human, hoping this meant they would play some more. However, she had to force her own voice to stay silent because of all the pain in her rump where the fire burned the worst.

When she'd finally made it out, she turned to see a fallen tree and lots of hot fire. She was on the edge of it, glad she didn't have to run. Her legs shook terribly, and her ears hardly worked.

"Come on!" she barked. "Get up!"

The human was covered in black marks, and some of her removable fur had the fire on them. She looked a lot different than she did a moment ago, though she smelled the same.

No, there was something different. Deogee sniffed until she figured it out. It was the smell of death.

"Not again!" she whined.

Deogee paced around her lost friend for a long time, saddened at how the fire had taken her, even as she figured out the kindly woman had probably given her life so that she might go on.

The fires were smoldering down to nothing when she finally got the courage to leave.

She limped over to the clothing of her prior friend. One sunrise ago, she and Melissa were walking the neighborhood, as they always did, and the human had disappeared mid-stride. All she'd left behind were the coverings she'd always used in place of fur. And those had blown into the nearby bushes, making it hard for her to remember her human's scent.

"Is it me?" she wondered. "Did I get my friendly humans killed?"

The world had been a noisy place, at least until Melissa went away. Now, it was silent, which spooked her.

"I don't want to be alone..."

Deogee walked around the property of the convent, barely noticing the white machine flying by as it left. She searched for another human she remembered as coming to the bad place before the fire struck.

There were four of them, and one of the youngest females slathered herself with a flowery scent. Deogee didn't particularly like it, but it was so powerful, she easily found it near the parking lot.

"She left the bad place," she thought. If she could get away from where two of her humans perished, so much the better.

"So nice of the girl to leave a trail."

She ran into the street, ignoring the pain of the burns.

Deogee made one stop at her friend Biscuit's house. She was the pretty black lab she and her human had briefly freed a short time earlier. She stood up on her hind legs and pressed the latch on the front door, as her human had done.

When the door opened, her loneliness went away.

No one was around to complain about all the playful barking.

Queens, NY

"Greetings, fellow human beings. I was once known as Dr. Jayden Phillips—a college professor, Nobel-prize-winning physicist, multi-million-selling self-help author, industrialist, and, my personal favorite, *Time* magazine's person of the year..." The man had long white hair down to his shoulders but wasn't that old; maybe fifty. His brown eyes and round face seemed relaxed, almost Zen, as he spoke.

"You know who he is?" he asked Emily during a pause in the guy's speech. The man looked extremely familiar, like he'd been on cable news channels many times before this, but Ted only caught the news while running through airports, so his recollection wasn't good.

"Mr. Phillips runs Southern Cross Industries," she replied. "They have their hand in everything—robotics, finance, computers, radio, space launches, and the guy's immense self-help publishing empire. He's been to the White House numerous times seeking tax breaks from President Tanager."

The man's speech continued, and he referenced himself as David and America as Goliath. He talked about taking down the nation and offering up the remains to the rest of the world. Then he gave his ultimatum to other countries to kick out the surviving citizens of the United States.

"Well, this seals it," Ted remarked when it looked like it was over. "We have to do something." It wasn't enough that this asshole had wiped out everyone on the continent. He wanted to finish the job overseas.

"Wait—" Emily leaned close to the television. "I don't think he's in the real Oval Office."

"Are you sure?" he said, glancing at the image.

"That's the wrong desk. Believe it or not, it's a big deal for a president to change where he sits. Several recent presidents sat at the *Resolute* desk. Tanager wanted to break with tradition, so he—"

"Built his own," Ted finished.

"You nailed it."

"So, is this guy in a replica Oval Office?"

"Almost certainly," she replied. "I've been to a few. It's one of those things VPs get to do. I take tours, get my picture taken with donors, and so on. I look like I'm doing something, you know?"

He acknowledged her, remembering his second-class role for so many years.

She went on. "There's a replica in the Bush Library in Texas. There's one in Virginia. Some private citizens have built their own. But I think this creep was broadcasting from Cheyenne Mountain, in Colorado."

"NORAD?"

"Yes. I've been there on one of my tours." She chuckled as if remembering those simple times. "But it's underground, so the curtains on the windows have to be drawn, like we just saw. And, if you really pay attention, the light never looks quite right outside the drapes. That's because it's fake."

"Wow. You have an eye for detail."

She patted her hair as if trying to get it to look perfect. "Trust me, when you're in the public eye twenty-four/seven, and they take endless photos, you take notice of good and bad light."

He'd gotten his photo taken on Air Force Two, just after saving her life. He couldn't imagine having someone pop out of the closet every time something important happened. "Sounds like a lower circle of Hell if you ask me."

Emily shrugged.

The speech ended and the signal faded back to the colored bars on the screen, prompting Ted to wonder how the transmission reached them in the first place. "If he killed everyone in these homes, why is this guy talking to us?"

She seemed to think on it. "We saw all those people in Newark. Maybe he's talking to them, but we're in the same viewing area."

He paced across the room. "Yeah. They're trying to take over. They've somehow snuck in while we were busy dying. But this signal had to be sent with the help of technicians at the cable company, right? Someone has to be monitoring things there. Maybe we can hunt them down and confirm this David guy is transmitting from NORAD. If we can take him out..."

Emily gave him a sideways look. "Just the two of us?" She got out her fake pen and paper. "Note to self: subject wants to win war single-handedly."

Ted smirked but didn't let her diminish his enthusiasm for solving the riddle. He followed the wires from behind the television to what he assumed was going to be a cable box. However, they went to a small white piece of equipment painted with a fancy S logo. "Oh, snap. This isn't a cable television."

"Satellite?" she asked.

"Not satellite, exactly. You said this guy was into everything. I don't suppose he was in with Southern Solar, was he?"

"I think so. Yes. All of his companies have the word southern in them. His publishing company was Southern Stacks, or something. I think his wife is from New Zealand and he likes things from south of the equator. Why? What are you thinking?"

He organized his thoughts. "I know what radio station we've been hearing the past couple of days. It isn't Super One Hundred, like I said before. It's Southern One Hundred, which is run by a company called Southern Solar, which also runs the digital TV service we've been watching. I thought they were different radio stations as we moved from city to city, but it was always the same one. The transmitter for S-O-H, FM, covers many states. That's because it isn't a normal radio station. It broadcasts from high in the air on multiple autonomous flying solar platforms."

As a pilot, he was aware of the numerous solar aircraft that plied the skies without ever landing, but they were seventy thousand feet in the air. Far above the commercial and military lanes he flew.

"I've heard of those. They stay in the air for years at a time."

"Yep. They have wingspans longer than a football field, and there's a whole fleet of them up there. I bet he owns most of them."

She snapped her fingers like he was on to something. "He kept the radio playing because he owns the transmitter."

"He's consolidated his position. Moved to the central US..." Ted knew he sounded deflated, because knowing who killed the nation wouldn't bring back those children he and Emily saw in the city. "And a guy with his resources could probably figure out what to do with the nuclear briefcase. I bet Ramirez took it right to him."

She exhaled, then grabbed his hand. "Sit down, please." She pointed to the sofa.

"What?" he remarked as he crashed onto the couch like a pallet of bricks.

"Ted, just listen," she insisted.

He did as she asked, then, based on her impatient tone, looked up at her with reservation. It seemed like she might scold him, possibly because she'd figured out he was winging this whole operation.

Emily stood in front of him but leaned close. She looked him in the eyes with a mix of sorrow and gratitude, then gave him a peck on the lips, taking him wildly by surprise.

"What the? Ma'am? What—"

Emily laughed. "I know things look bad outside, but we're not going to win the war with you falling asleep on your feet. You crash here on the couch. I'll take the little bed in the other room." She stood up straight. "And thanks for giving me space today when we found my husband. That's why I kissed you. Tomorrow, I might even hold your hand and be seen with you in public."

He was at a loss for what to say.

Emily pulled out her fake notebook. "Dear diary, I found out how to make Major Ted MacInnis go totally silent. A first."

That broke the logjam in his mind, and he let go with a hearty laugh.

Ted leaned back on the couch, content to survive another day.

Kyla was alive, too.

And he now knew who was going to pay for destroying the country. David what's-his-name might have thought he was safe from retaliation, but he wasn't. No matter how long it took, Ted intended to find out how he'd killed everyone. Then, it was time for payback.

That fight would start after some well-deserved rest.

###

To Be Continued in *Minus America*, Book 3

If you enjoyed this book, please leave a review. As you probably know, reviews are like high-octane fuel for independent authors such as me. The more I get, the better I'm doing in the eyes of Amazon. They then help promote the books doing better in reviews...

Thank you!

I have a short author note to follow.

COPYRIGHT

This book is a work of fiction.

All of the characters, organizations, and events portrayed in this novel are either products of the author's imagination or are used fictitiously. Sometimes both.

Empty Cities (and what happens within / characters / situations / worlds)

are Copyright (c) 2019 by E.E. Isherwood

Paperback Version 2.1 [3.17.23]

Cover by Covers by Christian

Editing by Mia at LKJ Books

AUTHOR NOTES

Written July 9, 2019

Thank you for reading book 2. At the risk of coming across with the musical grace of a dinner triangle, I hope you can take a moment to review this book on Amazon. Each review puts me closer to success, no matter how many reviews are already out there for this book. So, I'll take a minute to pause this note while you crank that out...

All good? Thank you!

I love the element of randomness in my books. You never know what's going to be around the next corner, and, I hope, characters experience challenges and behave in ways that might surprise you. I got a kick out of Dwight's decision to sit in the crosswalk, because he thought he was invisible. And being guided by an imaginary bird was another piece that just seemed to fit him.

If everyone around us disappeared one day, I'd guess we'd all have some unique takes on what might have caused it.

Speaking of causes, we now know a little about who was behind the attack on America, though not why, or how. One of my poorest reviews for book 1 complained that I did not reveal the details of the attack up front. That's a fair criticism, but I prefer to let the characters discover things on their own, and because I like to follow events in near real-time, it wouldn't fit the story if they wrapped up all the mystery in the first twenty-four hours. Like any good conspiracy, it must be unwrapped in layers.

On a related point about cause and effect, and as a student of history, I often wonder if humanity has ever developed a major weapon that it did not later use in warfare. We've used chemical weapons of the worst kind in the First World War. We've excelled at biological warfare (poisoning wells since antiquity, throwing plague-ravaged bodies at the enemy in the Middle Ages, and using bombs filled with fleas carrying bubonic plague during the 1940s). We've also harnessed and then weaponized the atom to destroy entire cities.

The scale of destruction has gone ever upward, so creating a weapon capable of destroying a continent can't be far away. We're going to need some good guys keeping watch on those military science experiments, don't you think?

Is that a hint? A look behind the Wizard of Oz's curtain? We shall see.

I hope you are enjoying the summer and keeping cool. Here in Missouri, the weather has been its usual unpredictable self. We've had more rain than we've had in years; the rivers ran over many of the roads near my house. Now, it's just hot and muggy. Too hot to get on my bike, which is killing me.

A special thanks to all the beta readers who have made each book even better.

Well, I've got to get back to it.

Thank you for reading,

EE

BACK MATTER

EE Isherwood's Back Catalog at a Glance

Neighborhood Watch Series – Frank retires to a quiet street in sunny Florida, but when the EMP strikes, his retirement is over. Now he must help his neighborhood survive the coming collapse of...everything. (7+ books)

Minus America Series – What would happen if everyone in the US vanished in a flash? Every trucker. Every housewife. Every police officer. Piles of clothes are all that remain. How would you survive in the empty land? And who would come to take it? Five books in this series.

End Days Series (co-written with Craig Martelle) – A post-apocalyptic adventure about a father and son on opposite ends of a continent ravaged by a failed EMP-like science experiment. Six books in this series.

Sirens of the Zombie Apocalypse Series – A teen boy must keep his great-grandma alive to find the cure to the zombie plague, but what if the only people immune are those over 100? They are always the first to die when the world breaks... Seven, soon to be eight books in this series.

Impact Series – A post-apocalyptic thriller about an asteroid of untold wealth slamming across the heartland of America. A Kentucky father must cross the devastation to find his daughter while others rush to exploit the space rock. Six books in this series. (Currently unpublished, relaunch soon)

Website

My updated website now has links to my back catalog on Amazon, so you can see all of them on one easy-to-read page. I've also got links to maps of my books, Kickstarter projects, a Patreon page, and you can sign up to my monthly newsletter.

Please visit www.eeisherwood.com for everything happening in my universe.

QUIET REFLECTIONS

Made in United States
Orlando, FL
28 January 2024

43018511R00235